KILLER PIZZA

KILLER PIZZA

a novel by
GREG TAYLOR

SCHOLASTIC INC.
New York Toronto London Auckland
Sydney Mexico City New Delhi Hong Kong

ISBN 978-0-545-24183-0

12 11 10 9 8 7 6 5 4 3 2
10 11 12 13 14 15/0

Printed in the U.S.A.   40

First Scholastic printing,
January 2010

Design by
Barbara
Grzeslo

PROLOGUE:
SOMETHING WICKED . . .

Run! Don't look back! Just run!!!

Charging through the dark woods, Chelsea Travers was already exhausted from running. She was also barefoot and unable to see more than a few feet in front of her, thanks to the dense canopy of trees overhead that prevented the moonlight from penetrating to the forest floor. Added up, three pretty big strikes against the fifteen-year-old, considering that she was running for her life.

"Help! Someone, please . . . HELP ME!"

Even as Chelsea cried out for help, she knew it was a stretch to think someone might hear her, way out here in the woods. But the words had suddenly burst out of her, as though she had no control over them.

You're losin' it, Chelsea thought as she ran between the trees. *You're totally losin' it! You have to keep it together.*

Or else you're dead!

Admitting the unthinkable to herself—that she might not get out of these woods alive—gave Chelsea a well-needed burst of adrenaline. She leaped over a fallen tree trunk, shot a wild glance over her shoulder, then continued her mad dash through the woods.

Thoughts buzzed in and out of Chelsea's brain as she ran.

What were you thinking, walking home alone through the woods at twelve o'clock at night?

Shoulda gone home with Lenny. So what if he was being a jerk, as usual?

What is this thing chasing me, anyway?!

More than anything, that's what had Chelsea so off-the-rails-I-can't-believe-this-is-happening terrified. The *not knowing* what was chasing her through the woods. The sudden snarling bursts, which shattered the nighttime silence behind her, obviously pointed to an animal of some sort. But Chelsea was certain she had glimpsed the thing on two legs as it ran after her. What kind of animal ran on two legs?

Suddenly, up ahead . . . a road! Chelsea couldn't believe her luck when she saw the ribbon of worn asphalt through the trees. She slapped aside branches as she sprinted for the two-laner, her heart pounding from fear and fatigue and I-just-might-make-it optimism.

But when Chelsea broke from the woods, she stumbled on the uneven terrain between the trees and the road, twisted her right ankle, and fell heavily to the ground. Slowly pulling herself to her feet, Chelsea limped to the middle of the road. To her right, darkness. To her left, at the bottom of a long hill . . . the red and blue lights of a gas station.

Civilization! But never had civilization felt so far away. Chelsea began a slow, hopeful, hobbled jog down the hill, carefully scanning the woods as she went. She hadn't gone very far before a searing flash of pain exploded in the back of her thigh.

Screaming in surprise—she hadn't heard even a whisper of warning that something was behind her—Chelsea whirled to defend herself. Her eyes widened when she saw what was standing in the middle of the road, towering over her. The light from the gas station wasn't bright enough to illuminate the huge thing's features, but it was obvious to Chelsea that she wasn't looking at any kind of animal. Not one *she'd* ever seen before, anyway.

What is that? Chelsea wondered, her head suddenly spinning. She felt like she'd been injected with some kind of sedative. As much as she urged herself to fight, to run, to do *something* to get away from the silent, bizarre creature that had bitten her, all Chelsea could do was sink to both knees. She was going fast and she knew it. The next thing she knew she was lying on the asphalt road, still warm from the hot June sun that had set three hours earlier.

The creature stepped toward Chelsea, its foot filling her fuzzy—and quickly fading—field of vision.

Bare feet. Long, deformed toes. And . . . what was that, a *toe ring*? Is that what Chelsea was seeing?

Strange . . .

That was Chelsea's confused last thought. Then her eyes closed and her world shut down.

PART ONE:
KILLER PIZZA

1

Toby Magill had just sat down at his desk to boot
up his computer when he heard his cell phone ring.
Tossing aside the graphic novels and clothes strewn
across his bedroom floor, Toby found the phone in a
pair of cargo shorts and snapped it open.

"Hello?"

"I'd like to speak to Toby Magill, please."

"I'm Toby."

"This is Steve Rogers, from Killer Pizza."

"Oh, yeah. Hi."

"I have good news, Toby. We'd like you to wear Killer
Pizza's distinctive black T-shirt with the red logo known
around the world."

"You would?"

"Congratulations. The job is yours to lose. Come in
tomorrow morning at eleven. By the end of the day you'll
know how to make the best pizzas in the *universe*."

Steve Rogers hung up before Toby had a chance to say thank you. Staring at the phone, Toby wondered if he really heard what he thought he had just heard. After peppering at least a dozen local businesses with work applications over the past few weeks—and getting turned down by all of them—had this man actually offered him a *job*?

If so, Toby wanted to do more than just say thank you to Steve Rogers. He wanted to kiss the guy's foot! He felt like letting out a whoop of joy! But Toby—by nature a shy, introverted kind of kid—bypassed the whoop of joy and simply smiled at this wonderful news.

So long, summertime blues!

Only two weeks had ticked by since school let out, but Toby was already dealing with a mean case of the SBs. Sure, he had his graphic novels, computer, video games, and chores he was always forgetting to do. But step outside of his home and there was *nothing to do* in his Ohio suburban community of Hidden Hills. Nothing for Toby, anyway. His only real friend had left for California to spend the summer with his dad and stepmother. That had left Toby hangin' out in the wind. Alone.

But this was great! Toby was confident that Killer Pizza would kick-start what had so far been an incredibly dull summer.

"Guess what? I got a job," Toby announced at dinner that evening.

Toby's mother frowned, obviously not overjoyed at the prospect of her son finding employment. His sister, Stacey, looked like she didn't believe him. As for Mr. Magill, Toby's news of summer employment brought a smile to his face. "That's great, Toby. Where?"

"Killer Pizza. It's right down on Industrial Avenue."

"Weird spot for a pizza place," Stacey said.

Toby felt like giving his bratty twelve-year-old sister a swift kick under the table. To say the two had a combative relationship would be putting it mildly.

It didn't help that Stacey was so *good* at everything, from academics to learning the flute to being so naturally at ease with people.

By contrast, nothing had ever come easily to Toby. He struggled to keep a B average, had not been able to master any of the instruments he had tackled so far—including his battered secondhand guitar—and had always found it difficult to make friends, thanks to that shy streak of his.

Those weren't the only differences between brother and sister. Physically they were worlds apart, as well, Stacey being a small, petite kid—she took after her mom in that regard—compared to Toby, who was big for his age and close enough to being overweight that his mother was constantly reminding him to watch those sweets.

"Well, that's where it is," Toby told his sister, referring to the location of Killer Pizza. "Go look for yourself if you don't believe me."

"I still think you're too young to be working," Mrs. Magill said. Toby had turned fourteen just a few months before, which meant he had been able to apply for a work permit. "Especially at a place called Killer Pizza. What kind of name is that?" Mrs. Magill's expression looked like she had just eaten something very distasteful.

"It's 'Pizza to Die For.' If I'm lucky, no one will die from any of the pizzas I make."

"*Toby!* That's a terrible thing to say!"

"Just a little joke, Mom. Anyway . . ." Toby gave his dad a smile as he got up from the table. "I start tomorrow morning." After placing his plate, silverware, and glass into the dishwasher, Toby walked from the room.

"Tell you one thing," Stacey yelled after her brother. "I'm not ordering a pizza from you, that's for sure!"

■ ■ ■

Stacey was actually right about Killer Pizza's address. It *was* an odd spot for a pizza place. Industrial Avenue wasn't an avenue at all. It was a dead-end side road lined with old, somewhat decaying industrial buildings that housed a hodgepodge of businesses, from Washabaugh Auto Body to a dog obedience school to Harr's Boat Covers.

Toby was nervous as he rode his bike past Harr's the following morning. "The job is yours to lose." That's what Steve Rogers had told him. When he got to the Killer Pizza shop—located in a crumbling, 1950s-era brick building that sported a certain kind of funky charm—he hesitated before entering, took a deep breath, then exhaled slowly.

Toby didn't want this job just to ward off the summertime blues. Fact was, he harbored a secret passion he hadn't revealed to anyone. Not to his family. Not to his best friend.

He religiously watched the Food Channel.

Yes, Toby thought it might be kind of cool to be a chef. And why not? Celebrity chefs were *in*, after all. They were stars. What they mostly *weren't*—from what Toby had seen on TV, anyway—were muscled, perfect-looking, athletic types, the kind who always brushed past him disdainfully in the hallways at school.

That gave Toby the license to dream about being a

chef in a way that he could never dream about being one of the Popular Kids at school. Problem was, dreaming was all Toby had done, as far as being a chef was concerned. Cooking was still a secret ambition of his, which meant he had zilch experience in the kitchen.

So *that's* why Toby was so nervous as he stood on the sidewalk in front of Killer Pizza. This wasn't dreaming anymore, it was real life, a pretty scary thing for someone who was not exactly overloaded with self-confidence. After squelching a sudden impulse to turn and run, Toby squared his shoulders and nodded. Ready or not, it was time. Time to meet his destiny!

Or at least try to learn how to make a decent pizza pie.

When Toby pushed through the front door of the pizza shop, he was greeted by the sight of four people standing in the small area in front of the ordering counter. He tried not to stare at the beautiful girl with the ink-black hair.

This can't be right, Toby thought. *That's Annabel Oshiro. What's she doing here?*

And yet it was Annabel Oshiro. A bona fide member of the Cool Kids Clique at Toby's school, Annabel was also a Rich Kid, her family being one of the wealthiest in the community. Impressive social credentials, to be sure, but the really impressive thing about Annabel—as far as Toby was concerned—was how down-to-earth she was. With her outgoing personality and winning smile, Annabel managed the rare feat of actually being nice to *everyone*, no matter where they were on the social scale.

Thrilled as Toby was at the prospect of working with Annabel, he couldn't help but wonder . . . why she was *here*, at Killer Pizza, standing in front of the large, colorful poster that advertised the various KP pizza choices. Certainly she had better, more exciting things to do than slave away in the hot kitchen of a take-out pizza chain all summer long.

"Mr. Magill?" Steve Rogers, with his crew cut, glasses, and *pressed T-shirt*, was the classic small-shop manager type. His eyes, magnified behind his glasses, were staring at Toby. "I'd like you to meet your fellow Killer Pizza staff."

Toby nodded, eager to get on with things.

Annabel smiled as she stepped toward Toby, holding out her hand. "You're Toby, right?"

"Yes," Toby said, surprised that Annabel knew his name.

"We had English and geometry together last year."

"Yes," Toby said again. He knew from taking those classes with Annabel that she was really smart, a serious student. So, let's see, in addition to being great-looking, popular, and one of the Rich Kids, Annabel was also a brainiac. Not a bad résumé.

"This should be fun," Annabel said, looking like she meant it.

"Yes," Toby said. *Better come up with a few more words in this conversation or this girl's gonna think you're an idiot!*

A tall guy with a lean but muscular build was the next one to shake Toby's hand. "Strobe," he said simply. Strobe had really intense green eyes, Toby noticed, eyes that seemed to take him in and size him up in a quick glance. Unlike Annabel's warm greeting, Strobe's was cool, abrupt. Toby didn't recognize him. Strobe—whatever kind of name that was—looked older to Toby. Which would explain his unfamiliarity. He probably went to Triple H (Hidden Hills High), the intimidating fortress that Toby would begin attending in the fall.

"And, last but not least, this is Doug," Steve said, indicating a teenager who looked like he wanted to be anywhere else but in the front reception area of Killer Pizza. Doug did not respond to Toby's effort to shake hands. After holding out his hand awkwardly for a moment, Toby withdrew it. *Okay, this kid is kinda strange.*

"You four are the first employees of the Hidden Hills franchise of Killer Pizza," Steve announced. Toby thought Steve might tear up, he looked so emotional. "Wear the colors proud."

With that, Steve distributed four Killer Pizza T-shirts and four Killer Pizza baseball-style caps. The T-shirts were black with KILLER PIZZA on the front pocket in small, red letters. On the back of the tee—also in red— was a large, smiling, Godzilla-like creature holding up a steaming pizza pie. Beneath this variation on the Italian chef holding up a pizza was the KP logo . . .

PIZZA TO DIE FOR.

"What do you say, people?" Steve said, his eyes glinting with excitement. "Let's learn how to make pizzas!"

■ ■ ■

Toby fell backward onto his bed that evening and smiled up at the ceiling. *Yes!* He had passed the first test!

True, he had no idea how he would react under fire, during the busy dinner hours when he would have to choose from more than two dozen toppings and three different types of dough as he quickly constructed one of five different sizes of specialty pizzas after another (example: the Creature Double Feature—two medium-size pizzas, choice of any three toppings). But so far, so good.

Toby had absolutely loved the feel of the dough between his hands as he began making his first pizza. He loved the challenge of sprinkling just the right amount of ingredients onto the round pie. (They were all instructed to make a Monstrosity—an extra large with everything.)

Finally, there was the nervous—but somehow wonderful—anticipation as he waited for his pie to come out of the wood-burning oven. When it did, Steve tasted Toby's first Killer Pizza. He had criticized all the others for one reason or another. "Too much pepperoni" (Strobe's). "Too doughy" (Annabel's). "This is a total disaster!" (Doug's).

So Toby had waited to see what was wrong with his pizza. He knew something had to be wrong with it. But then Steve, his eyes closed for what seemed like a long time after tasting Toby's pizza, looked at him and said, "This pizza . . . is *killer*!"

Toby smiled, thinking of that moment. It was a moment he had a hard time believing had really happened. But it had. It really had. Heck, who knew, could be he was a *natural* at this. Could be he was *too good* for Killer Pizza. Of course, he'd work there for a while, get some experience, but then . . . he'd strike out on his own! Open his own pizza shop! Write a bestselling pizza cookbook! Have his own show on the FC!

"How bad was your first day, on a scale of one to ten?" Toby hadn't noticed Stacey, arms crossed, smug smile, leaning against the jamb in his open bedroom doorway. Toby felt so good he didn't even mind that Stacey had interrupted his delicious pizza dreams. He calmly got up from his bed and walked toward his sister.

"On a scale of one to ten, ten being best? It was an *eleven*!" Toby slammed the door in Stacey's face, then smiled when he heard her run off down the hall, calling out for her mom as though she were a five-year-old. Turning away from the door, Toby walked over to his open window.

The view didn't look as tired as it did the day before. The hills of Hidden Hills now seemed to glow brightly in the amber light of the setting sun. Toby leaned on the sill and breathed in the warm, humid evening air. Incredible how things could change so quickly. From dreading the summer to suddenly welcoming it with open arms!

Wait, what was that?

Toby frowned as he scanned the line of trees that bordered the backyard of his house. He had just seen something move through those trees. A large upright shape of some sort, too large to have been human.

What was *that?* Toby wondered. *A bear? Is that what I just saw?* Toby wasn't even sure if there were bears anywhere around Hidden Hills. Besides that, he was *pretty* sure they didn't jog around on two legs.

A sudden breeze blew through the trees. The movement of the leaves shimmering in the dying summer light caused Toby to snap back to reality. The shape in the woods was probably nothing. Probably just a trick of lighting.

Turning away from the window, Toby plopped himself back onto his bed. He was anxious to get back to his Killer Pizza dreams.

Still, as Toby lay on his bed, he couldn't quite shake the image of the shape in the woods. *Had* it been a trick of lighting? Or simply leaves moving in a summer breeze?

Yeah, of course it was, Toby convinced himself. Then, starting with when he rode his bike up to Killer Pizza at eleven o'clock, Toby ran through the events of his wonderful day one more time.

2

Several hours after Toby was distracted by the
mysterious shape outside his house, a young employee
of Hidden Hills Echo 8-Plex movie theater exited the rear
doors of the theater and walked toward his '92 Corolla. It
was well past midnight and he had just finished his least
favorite chore, cleaning up the mess left behind in the
theaters after another long summer day of cinematic
fun. The kid pulled his keys out of his pocket and was
about to open his car door when he felt a sharp sting of
pain at the back of his thigh.

"OWWWWW!!!"

Dropping his keys as he spun around, the kid was so
startled at what he saw behind him that he froze on the
spot, mouth open in astonishment.

"What the . . ."

A streetlamp shone brightly behind the figure standing a few feet away, obscuring its features but sharply defining its tall, monstrous shape. If the kid had any impulse to run away from the thing, he wasn't able to act on it. He staggered suddenly from the effects of the bite, tried to stay upright, but fell backward and landed on his butt. He slowly looked up at the creature that had taken a step toward him, his expression registering confusion and disbelief.

"What is this, a joke?"

The thing—*whatever* it was—did not reply to the question. The kid did a kind of slow-motion tilt—his eyes never leaving the incredible sight in front of him—then collapsed onto his side. He seemed to be trying to say something, but his voice was low and slurred.

The creature remained standing a few feet away, silently studying its prey. It only took a few more moments for the kid's eyes to close, then he lay still on the concrete.

3

On Killer Pizza's opening day, Toby woke up long before he needed to. Actually, he felt like he hadn't slept more than a few minutes the entire night, he was so excited.

And nervous. He had spent the past few days with Annabel, Strobe, and Doug training at the shop, honing his pizza-making skills and learning everything from the right words to say when answering the phone to the proper way to clean up shop.

When the time came for Toby to hop onto his bike and pedal down the street to Industrial Avenue, he checked himself out in the mirror one last time. The uniforms kids were forced to wear for their summer jobs were usually pretty embarrassing. But Killer Pizza's black tee and baseball cap—complemented with blue jeans and black Converse sneakers—wasn't the least bit embarrassing. It was downright cool, Toby thought. He nodded at his image in the mirror, sucked in his gut—yeah, that was better—then headed off to his first day at work, saying a silent prayer that everything would go smoothly.

■ ■ ■

"*Stop* it, you two!"

Toby and Strobe interrupted their argument as soon as they heard Annabel's command. However Toby had imagined what day one might be like, this particular scenario had never crossed his mind. He and Strobe had been butting heads in the kitchen from the moment Killer Pizza opened.

Maybe it was the name, Killer Pizza. Or the corny but fun names of the various pizza and side order choices. (In addition to the Creature Double Feature and Monstrosity pizzas, KP also featured a Fangtastic Hawaiian pizza, Beasties—little bite-size pizzas, the Frankensausage pie, and Vampire Stakes—pointed garlic sticks with red dipping sauce.)

Or perhaps people were intrigued by the unusual location of the place. Whatever the reason, opening day of the Hidden Hills Killer Pizza franchise had been *crazy* since it opened its doors. Steve had led them to believe it would be a quiet day. That they would have time to develop their pizza legs, so to speak.

So much for Steve's crystal-ball prediction. Annabel, Toby, and Strobe had been taking phone order after phone order and making one pizza after another for more than three hours. They were struggling to keep things together and were already exhausted from the pace.

Doug had been no help whatsoever. Matter of fact, he had already proven himself to be a liability. In just a few short hours he had botched a couple of phone orders, put wrong ingredients on one of the pizzas, and spilled an entire gallon jar of pizza sauce on the kitchen floor. His coworkers already wanted to strangle him.

"If we don't get some organization here we might as well close up shop and go home," Annabel said, her face glistening with sweat from the kitchen heat.

"No kidding," Strobe shot back. "Where's Steve, anyway?" (He'd left shortly after opening the shop and hadn't come back.)

"I don't know," Annabel replied. "But it seems we can't count on him."

"This is *weird*." Strobe paced back and forth in the small kitchen. "Why would the guy just bolt like that? He's the manager!"

"It doesn't matter, Strobe!" That was Toby's reply, which certainly didn't help ease the tension that crackled between the two of them.

Whoa, take it easy, Toby urged himself. He couldn't remember the last time he'd gotten into an argument with someone other than his sister. It signaled to Toby just how stressed he was on his first official day at work, how quickly things had gotten out of control.

Just then the phone rang. Annabel went to answer it, but Doug had been sitting like a slug right next to the old-fashioned, 1950s-era black telephone—the entire shop was decorated with a kind of '50s vibe—and already had the receiver in his hand.

"It's clear that Toby's the fastest at making pizzas," Annabel said when she returned to the kitchen. "I think he should be head chef. That means anything dealing with food, he gives the orders."

Toby was shocked to hear Annabel say that. It was true, he was the fastest at making pizzas, but head chef? He would have never suggested that.

"Wait a second," Strobe countered. "I'm not a half bad doughboy myself."

"I didn't say you weren't," Annabel said. "But we need someone in charge."

"So who put you in charge of deciding who's in charge?"

"Gimme a break, Strobe. I'm just trying to sort things out here."

"I think Strobe should be head chef," Toby said. He simply didn't have the confidence to take on such a responsibility. But instead of saying that, Toby added, "After all, he's the oldest one here."

That much was true. Strobe was fifteen, Toby and Annabel fourteen, and Doug . . . well, no one was sure how old Doug was. He acted like a preschooler, as far as his coworkers were concerned.

"Okay," Annabel said. "If that's what you want, Toby. Strobe's in charge here in the kitchen."

"Thank you, Annabel," Strobe said, his voice laced with sarcasm.

Actually, Toby hadn't said what he really thought. Which was . . . *Annabel* should be in charge. She had proven herself to be a very calm, very efficient worker. Plus she got along with everyone.

As for Strobe . . . Toby simply wasn't sure what to make of him. He didn't talk much. Just came in, did the work, left at the end of the day with an abrupt "see ya." Strobe made Toby uncomfortable, that's for sure. He seemed to be . . . well, a pretty angry guy. What Strobe had to be angry about, Toby had no idea. But it made him want to step lightly around the kitchen's new head chef. He didn't want to get on Strobe's bad side. Speaking of which . . .

"What about *this* slacker?" Strobe growled when Doug walked into the kitchen with the phone order he had just written down. Concerned that Strobe might actually pop the timid Doug, Annabel stepped between the two of them.

"Doug?" Annabel said. "I have a really good job for you." Doug just stared back at Annabel. "If you could take the pizzas, once they've been removed from the oven, and place them in the cardboard boxes, that would be great."

Doug looked like he was tackling one of the great riddles of the universe. When he finally nodded, Annabel turned back to Strobe and Toby. "I'll answer the phone and handle the cash register, keep the kitchen clean, make pizzas when needed. If we find that we need another person to help, I'll talk to Steve about that. Okay?"

Toby nodded. Strobe had already turned to scrutinize the order Doug had placed on the revolving wheel above the counter. "Genius!" he called out to Doug, who had disappeared down a hallway that led to the bathroom, Steve's office, and the storage room. "You sure they ordered a dozen Mummy Wraps?!"

■ ■ ■

The errant Steve arrived back at the shop later that night, just before the older kids arrived to take over the nine to one A.M. shift. He entered to find three exhausted, practically-dead-on-their-feet employees. As for Doug . . . he'd already left the building.

Ignoring the comatose looks on his employees' faces, Steve gave everyone a big grin. "Ready to do this all over again tomorrow?"

4

Toby was riding his bike home from work later that evening when he heard the sound.

He stopped in the middle of Hazel Street, not far from his house, and looked toward the woods that stretched out behind the row of split-level brick houses to his right. The sound had been a strange animal-like howl, unlike anything Toby had ever heard before. And he'd spent a lot of time in those woods, too, especially when he was younger.

Toby shivered suddenly. Couldn't have been from the evening breeze. The night air was warm and humid. So why did Toby feel as though a chill had just run right through him? He remembered the mysterious shape he had seen behind his house after his first day of training at Killer Pizza. This was the first time he had thought about it since that night.

Snap out of it! Toby told himself. *The sound was just an animal of some sort.*

Still, Toby felt a sudden urgency to get home. He stood up on his bike pedals and pumped briskly up the hill. After stashing his bike in the garage, he talked briefly to his parents about his first official day at work, then took a shower and retired to his bedroom.

Just before going to bed, Toby went to his window to take a look out at the dark woods. When he was younger, Toby had often imagined strange beings lurking under his bed, or in his closet, or outside . . . in those dark woods. But Toby was fourteen years old now. He'd grown out of his monster phase a long time ago.

Just the same, Toby was not displeased at the lack of activity in the woods that rose up beyond his backyard. With a final glance at the dark landscape, he pulled down his window, closed the shutters, and got into bed. It was only ten o'clock but Toby was totally drained—physically and mentally—from the long, difficult first day at Killer Pizza.

Which meant it didn't take long for Toby to drift off to sleep. But just before his brain shut down for the night, Toby was sure that he heard that sound again— that odd animal-like howl—off in the distance.

5

"One Fangtastic Hawaiian!"

Strobe slid the pizza into its cardboard box and took it to the counter, where a couple of Triple H girls were waiting to take it outside. Killer Pizza was take-out only, but Steve had decided to install a few tables, with umbrellas to ward off the summer sun, on the sidewalk since opening day two weeks ago. They were always full. Business was good.

Fortunately, after a rough start, Toby, Annabel, and Strobe had managed to get their "pizza legs" and were handling the busy lunch and dinner hours much better than they had the first week.

"Thanks, Strobe!" the two girls said. Strobe nodded and went back to the kitchen. He was studying the order forms on the revolving wheel when Annabel said, "I've been wondering about something, Strobe."

Strobe gave Annabel a look. *Yeah?*

"Where'd that nickname come from?"

At first Annabel wasn't sure Strobe was going to answer the question. Then he said, "My dad started calling me that when I was a kid. Said I reminded him of one. Light one moment. Dark the next."

Haven't seen the light side yet, Toby thought as he prepared a Creature Double Feature with garlic, spinach, and black olives. The past two weeks hadn't done much to change his initial impression of Strobe, which was not good. Toby was working better with him in the kitchen, that much was true, and he had actually exchanged more than a few words with him over the past week, but Strobe continued to be a cool, closed-off character. Toby still didn't feel very comfortable being around him.

Annabel, however, seemed determined to break through Strobe's tough exterior. She was beginning to make some progress, Toby thought. Strobe definitely talked to her more than to him.

"Know what?" Annabel said. "I've never had a nickname."

"Maybe you're just not a nickname kinda girl," Strobe countered.

"Just don't call me Annie. No, I think my parents are too formal for anything like that. As for my friends . . .

well, the less said about them the better. How about you, Toby?"

"What?"

"What do your friends call you?"

"Nothing," Toby said a little too quickly. He had actually been saddled with a cruel nickname when he was younger and a bit more on the heavy side, but he wasn't about to mention that. Strobe was giving him a lingering, suspicious look, so to deflect attention he said, "Why the less said about your friends the better, Annabel?"

"I don't know. They've been kinda weird ever since I started working here. They don't get it, I guess. Neither does my dad, for that matter. Order of Vampire Stakes!" Annabel relayed to the outside tables over a kitchen intercom.

"What don't they get?"

Annabel held up a finger. *Be right back.* After delivering the garlic sticks and returning to the kitchen, Annabel indicated her T-shirt and cap. "*This*, for one thing."

"Get out. Your friends don't like your KP cottons?"

"Are you kidding? It's a *uniform*. Only thing worse than that, as far as they're concerned, is my choice to be here instead of hanging out at the pool with them."

33

"Total immersion in a cool pool sounds pretty good to me right now," Strobe said.

"As for my dad," Annabel continued, "he doesn't understand why I would want to work here instead of at one of *his* stores. He almost didn't sign my work permit."

"What kind of stores?" Strobe asked.

"Business furniture and supplies."

"Hey, I'll work at one of his stores. With commissions? Has to pay better than here. But then, you don't have to worry about money, do you, Annabel?"

"There you go," Annabel said, fixing Strobe with an annoyed frown. "So typical."

"What?" Strobe asked, looking genuinely perplexed.

"You just stamped a label on my forehead. Rich brat, right?"

"No, I was just saying . . ."

"Why do people have to do that? Put everyone in a box? People are more than just one thing, you know? That's *exactly* why I took this job. I wanted to do something different. Something unexpected. Why are *you* here, Strobe?"

Instead of being defensive at Annabel's sudden, uncharacteristic attack, Strobe looked amused. "I need to make money. How 'bout you?" Strobe was looking at

Toby. "Let's get this all out in the open. Why are you here?"

Toby didn't want to reveal anything about his chef dreams, so he decided to be totally honest. "This was the only job I could get."

"There you have it!" Strobe said with a sweep of his hand. "Now we all know why we're here. Okay, Annabel? We cool?"

Annabel studied Strobe for a moment. "Yeah, we're cool. Just don't . . ." Annabel flinched when Strobe grabbed a dish towel and wiped her forehead. "What? I'm a totally gross sweaty or something?"

"Just wipin' off that label. See anything on Annabel's forehead?"

What Toby saw was one incredibly great-looking fourteen-year-old. "No, I don't see a thing."

"Good. Nobody's gettin' put in a box in this kitchen." With that, Strobe headed out to the counter to take an order from a group of skater boys. When Toby exchanged a look with Annabel, she shrugged apologetically. "Sorry. Didn't mean to get all worked up."

"That's okay. Strobe shouldn't have said that about you."

"Maybe, but . . . I don't know . . . I have been kind of edgy lately. At home, anyway. With my friends."

"Why?"

Annabel hesitated. She looked like she wasn't sure if she wanted to continue talking about this. But then she said, "Don't laugh, okay?"

"Of course not."

"It's been kind of a gradual thing, actually. It's not like I woke up one morning and all of a sudden thought . . . I'm *changing*."

"Changing?"

Annabel nodded. "I feel like . . . well, like there's this other person inside me, itching to get out."

"What kind of person?" Toby was really interested. That's how *he'd* been feeling recently, what with his chef dreams and all.

Before Annabel could answer, a bell went off on the counter, signaling it was time to retrieve a couple of pizzas from the oven. As Toby and Annabel took out the Monstrosities, sliced them, and put them into their cardboard sleeves . . .

"So what were we talking about?" Annabel said.

"This alien inside of you."

"Right." Annabel thought for a moment, then said, "She's me, of course. But different. In some really important ways."

"How?"

"Well . . . for one thing, she definitely *did not* want to work at one of her dad's business supply stores this summer. Which, of course, she was expected to do. And she has no desire to take over the family business, or become a doctor or a lawyer or anything like that."

"Is that what your dad wants you to do?" Toby asked, surprised.

"The holy grail of his wish list for me."

"Wow, my dad was thrilled I was just able to land a summer job."

Annabel smiled. "That's the way it should be, right? We're only fourteen, after all." As Annabel started to clean up the kitchen counter she looked over at Toby. "Know what I think might have started all this? Wanting to break out of the box and all that?" Toby shook his head. "Remember that extra-credit assignment we had near the end of the year in English class?"

Toby had to think a moment, then nodded. It was an assignment he had passed on, the regular assignments being more than enough to keep him busy.

"I decided to trace my family's history for the assignment. I couldn't believe what I discovered. It turns out I'm related, I'm pretty sure about this, things got a little murky around the seventeenth century, but I'm pretty sure that I'm related to a sixteenth-century samurai!"

"Get out," Toby said, truly impressed with Annabel's revelation.

"I'm totally serious."

"Well, there you have it. No way would a samurai work at a business supply store."

"Exactly!" Annabel said with a laugh. "Or hang out at a pool, either."

"On the other hand, would he work at Killer Pizza?"

Annabel looked around the kitchen. It was a total mess after almost eight busy hours. She shrugged. "It's a start."

Toby and Annabel exchanged smiles, then fell silent as they got back to work, Annabel making quick progress in the messy kitchen, Toby putting together an order of Beasties, his final pizza assignment of the day.

Toby felt all warm inside as he worked, and it wasn't just from the hot kitchen. He was thrilled that Annabel had felt comfortable enough with him to reveal this other "color" of hers, a more searching, less confident side that she had buried beneath her more cheerful, self-assured exterior. Getting to know Annabel was one of the really terrific things about Killer Pizza, as far as

Toby was concerned. There were other things, to be sure.

Basically, Toby loved coming into work every day. He hadn't at first, during the first week when things had been so difficult. But then he and Annabel and Strobe—forget about Doug—had slowly settled in and figured out how to efficiently operate a busy pizza shop. In addition to the assignment of duties and the experience of just coming in and doing the job every day, the real breakthrough had been Strobe's idea to start playing music.

They had all—except for Doug—contributed ideas to a CD that Strobe put together. Toby had been especially pleased with one of his selections, an infectious punk/pop version of the 1960s classic "Monster Mash" by an unknown band he had discovered on the Internet. That song had survived the final elimination process, during which at least a dozen songs were tossed. The final playlist was all over the place, musically—classic rock, hip-hop, folkie rock—but somehow it worked. It was like all three of their personalities were on that Killer Pizza sound track. When the music had started pulsing over the KP speakers, everything suddenly jelled. From then on, the three of them had been a tight, efficient working unit. It felt great being part of it, Toby thought happily as he put the finishing touches on his Beasties.

Just then the evening shift came into the shop. Steve was right behind them, and Strobe was right behind Steve with the skater boys' orders.

"Where's Doug?" Steve asked curtly when he came into the kitchen.

"He had to leave early," Annabel said. "Something about a crisis at home."

"Come to my office, please."

The trio exchanged glances as Steve strode down the hallway and disappeared into his small, windowless office.

"Is it my imagination, or is he ticked off?" Toby asked.

"Maybe it was a mistake to let Doug leave," Annabel said.

"Doesn't matter," Strobe said. "The genius doesn't do anything, anyway. Let's go see what Steve has to say." Strobe walked down the hall toward Steve's office as the next group of pizza chefs started to get busy in the kitchen. Toby and Annabel nodded their hellos, then followed Strobe.

Steve was behind his desk, looking through a thick sheaf of papers as they filed in.

"Is there something wrong, Steve?" Annabel asked nervously.

"I'll let the owner of Killer Pizza decide that." Steve placed his papers neatly on the desk in front of him. "He always visits his franchises a few weeks after opening. To check the books, see how things are progressing. See if any changes are needed."

"I'd like to suggest a change," Strobe said. "Doug. Get rid of the guy. He's terrible."

Toby winced at Strobe's blunt assessment of their coworker. Steve leveled his gaze at Strobe. "I suggest you share your feelings about Doug with Mr. Major, Strobe. He'll be here in a few minutes. He wants to talk to the three of you." Steve got up from behind his desk. "Good luck."

Annabel hit Strobe on the arm as soon as Steve had left the room. "What were you *thinking*?"

"I spoke the truth, didn't I?"

"Sometimes it's better to hold back on the truth, Strobe. If Doug *is* related to Steve, or maybe even to this Mr. Major, you might have just found yourself the exit door."

"The owner of Killer Pizza isn't gonna fire me. I'm head chef, after all."

The door suddenly opened behind Toby, Annabel, and Strobe. The three did not look over their shoulders to greet the owner of Killer Pizza. They stared straight ahead at the wall behind the desk and waited for him to come around the desk and address them. What they saw gave them a bit of a shock.

Doug appeared before them, plopped down into Steve's chair, and propped his feet on the desk. "Hey, gang. How's it goin'?!"

6

Of course they thought it was a joke. Something cooked up between Steve and Doug. But *why*? Why pull such an elaborate stunt?

"I'd ask you to take a seat," Doug said. "But as you can see, there are none. We're on a bit of a shoestring budget here at Killer Pizza. I like to put my money where it's best needed."

Doug's transformation was truly remarkable. Gone was the perpetual slouch in his posture. The furtive look in his eyes. And the Killer Pizza T-shirt. Doug now wore a natty, perfectly tailored business suit.

"An explanation is obviously in order. What the three of you didn't realize is that these past few weeks have been a test. I like to observe my potential future employees up close and personal."

"Hold on!" Strobe interrupted. "What are you talking

about, test? What's going on here? You expect us to believe you're the owner of Killer Pizza?"

"You can believe what you want, Strobe, but the simple fact of the matter is . . . I am. Oh, and by the way? My real name is Harvey. Harvey P. Major. The third." Harvey P. Major III leaped nimbly to his feet and walked toward the door. "If you'll follow me, I'd like to show you something."

The trio exchanged can-you-believe-this looks before following Harvey out of the room. He led them down the hallway to the storage room—the room that housed the jars of pizza sauce and cans of condiments and the refrigerators stocked with the cheeses and pepperoni and tomatoes and all of the other fresh toppings that were the "lifeblood" of Killer Pizza. When they were gathered in the middle of the room, Harvey closed the door and locked it. Toby and Annabel looked at each other uneasily. What was going *on* here?

Harvey smiled. "All of this?" he said, indicating the storage room with a sweep of his hand. "Is a front. A legitimate front, mind you. We make darn good, award-winning pizzas at Killer Pizza. I take this business very seriously. But it was created for one reason, and one reason only. To fund my humanitarian work."

Harvey paused, allowing the trio time to ponder what kind of humanitarian work he was involved in.

"Which is?" Annabel asked.

"I eliminate monsters."

The statement hung in the room. It was as though letters had actually formed and floated in the air in front of Toby, Annabel, and Strobe.

I . . . eliminate . . . monsters.

Harvey turned and walked to a corner of the room. He took hold of the side of a shelf filled with Killer Pizza's award-winning sauce with the special, secret ingredient and pulled it toward him. *The shelf opened silently and easily, like a huge door!* In the opening created by the pizza-shelf door was a spiral staircase that led downward to an out-of-sight basement.

"Come!" Harvey said cheerfully, then disappeared down the stairs.

The three instinctively hung back. They stood together in the middle of the room, staring at the hidden staircase, then Strobe finally said, "Well, I'm game," and walked toward the opening.

"Strobe!" Annabel said. "Hold on a second. Let's think about this. I mean . . . a hidden staircase? Our boss, who we didn't know was our boss, reveals that his humanitarian work is killing monsters?"

"You're not taking him seriously, are you? Obviously this is just some kind of joke." Strobe resumed walking toward the opening in the corner of the storage room and headed down the stairs. Annabel and Toby gave each other a look, then fell in behind Strobe, with Toby bringing up the rear.

As he walked down the spiral staircase, Toby had a sudden panicked thought. What if the door behind him was thrown shut and locked? They'd be trapped in a basement room with their strange pizza boss!

Get a grip! Toby scolded himself. *Like Strobe said, this is just some kind of bizarro joke.*

Still, Toby felt goose bumps on his arms as he descended into the basement beneath the Killer Pizza shop. When he got to the bottom of the staircase he felt like turning around and heading right back up again. The whole downstairs scenario just felt so *wrong*.

The large basement room stretching out in front of Toby contained several spotless aluminum operating tables and scores of gleaming surgical utensils hanging from hooks on the walls. If that wasn't weird enough, there was the smell to accent the odd basement furnishings. *Formaldehyde?* Is that what it was?

Strobe and Annabel stood in front of Toby. From the

far end of the basement room, Harvey gave the trio a re-assuring smile. "Don't be alarmed. I'm not a miniature version of Hannibal Lecter. This is a forensics room. For conducting autopsies on deceased monsters."

Annabel gave Strobe a slow, sideways glance. Strobe didn't look *quite* as confident that an April Fool's–type joke was being pulled on them.

"Your obvious uneasiness and disbelief is to be ex-pected," Harvey continued. "Allow me to prove to you that I'm not a total, raving loon." Harvey turned to a high, narrow refrigerator located behind him and opened the door. The trio couldn't believe what they saw hang-ing from a hook in the fridge.

It was *a large, grotesque figure that looked like a cross between a human and an animal!*

This time the creature was not backlit by a street-lamp or shrouded in darkness. The bright basement light revealed every chilling detail of the thing's fea-tures.

A hairless, elongated head with a pronounced jaw. Eyes set in deep, dark sockets. Ears . . . well, the crea-ture *had* no ears. Chest, abnormally large even for its six-foot-tall frame. Fingers and toes, long and muscular and accented by sharp talons. Finally, there was the distinctive-looking skin. Tough as leather, it was irregularly spotted light and dark, camouflage-like.

The thing looked horrific. And incredibly dangerous.

"I bagged this guy a few days ago," Harvey revealed. "Come. It won't bite. Not now, anyway. If you had met it when I did, that would have been a different story."

The three teens didn't move. Actually, they looked as though they couldn't have moved even if they wanted to. They were too blown away by the sight in front of them.

"Very well," Harvey said. "I'll give you a briefing from here. In one form or another, monsters have been around for as long as we humans have. From the beginning, they've always done one of three things to us. Devoured us, sucked our blood, stolen our souls. Not necessarily in that order. The bottom line? They are not our friends. Take this creature, for example. His species has been around a very long time. Latin name, *Guttata horridus horridus*. Guttata, for short. The guttata are cousins, you might say, of the gargoyle. But unlike their more primitive gargoyle brethren, guttata have evolved into a very sophisticated species."

Feeling as though he had been enveloped by some kind of strange, numbing cloud, Toby watched Strobe approach the creature. Annabel fell in behind Strobe.

Toby didn't want to be left behind, so he followed Annabel.

"Our friend here shares certain characteristics with the vampire and werewolf," Harvey continued. "For example, if a human were to be bitten by a guttata, they would slowly transform into one of these creatures. Guttata have the ability to morph back and forth between human and guttata form. They prefer the human form. Which is how the guttata manage to walk among us. One could be your neighbor, for all you know."

Toby stared at Harvey. Someone he knew could be a guttata? How far left of Main Street was *that*? Strobe reached out and touched the creature, then rubbed his thumb against his fingers, as though feeling some sort of residue from his contact with the beast. "Could be a fake," he surmised.

"I assure you it's not," Harvey replied. "Listen, I know this is a bit much to lay on you all at once. Why don't we go to my office? Have some refreshments." Harvey indicated a door in the corner of the room. "I have photo albums. An introductory film on the monster universe. Various relics, mostly handed down from my father and grandfather, from their years of service protecting the unsuspecting public from the creatures of the night."

Strobe suddenly snorted a laugh. It was all so *absurd*, after all. Annabel, however, looked quite serious when she asked, "Harvey, let's say this thing is for real. Why are you showing us all this?"

"I'm sorry, Annabel. I thought it was obvious. I want you to work for me."

"We are working for you," Toby pointed out.

"Not making pizzas. I want you to consider becoming Killer Pizza MCOs."

"Which would be?" Strobe asked.

"Monster Combat Officers." With that, Harvey walked across the room and opened the door to his office. He stood to one side, waiting for the trio to join him.

7

A young female vampire, wearing a sleeveless T-shirt and plaid miniskirt, rushed at the video camera with fangs bared. . . .

A scraggly, gaunt werewolf—captured on old, grainy black-and-white film—leaped with incredible speed and power to the top of a garage in a dark back alley, glared at the camera, and disappeared into the darkness. . . .

A pack of ferocious guttata attacked a barricaded house, a half dozen of the creatures trying to get at the MCOs inside, who shouted commands and warnings to one another in a hard-to-place foreign language. Greek, maybe?

Those were just a few of the images on the film that Harvey showed Toby, Annabel, and Strobe in his office. There were quite a few others. An *avalanche* of images, revealing the strange and bizarre world of the creatures of the night, from the familiar (zombies, vampires, were-wolves) to the not so (nagas and MAPs—mind-altering parasites—among others).

When the film ended, Harvey turned the office lights back on. Strobe, Toby, and Annabel blinked, their eyes adjusting to the bright light. It was as though they had just returned to daylight from a very weird, indoor amusement park–like ride. The kind with the fake creatures that jump out at you from the darkness. The kind that scares the crap out of you, when you're younger.

But the creatures in Harvey's film had obviously not been fake. Nothing phony or CGI-like about them, whatsoever.

Harvey took a seat behind his desk and studied the trio. "Convinced now that this is not some kind of elaborate joke?" When there was no response to his question: "I'll take that as a yes. Which means I can proceed with my pitch. I hired the three of you to work at Killer Pizza because I sensed you each have something special to offer. Annabel, as I expected, you're a quick study. You have the ability to take things in, process them, and move on. You're extremely focused. It didn't take long for you to establish yourself as the bedrock of this team. That's because you have the posture of a true leader."

Harvey shifted his gaze to Strobe. "Strobe, you're a no-nonsense, hard worker. I like that. You're the *muscle* of this group, you might say. But you definitely have a temper. And a problem with authority. You have to watch that. I'll be keeping my eye on you if you decide to accept my offer here."

After hearing Harvey's assessment of his two coworkers, Toby was curious. What did *he* have to offer?

"Toby, you're the perfect balance to these two. You're low-key, you take orders well. A necessary quality in any officer. I don't mean that as a slight. You do good work, you pay attention to the details. That's important. Besides, I believe you have qualities you don't even realize yet. You just need some seasoning. Pun intended."

Harvey leaned back in his seat and looked at his three KP employees. "The point here is that I believed the three of you would make a good team. I'm rarely wrong about things like that, and I certainly wasn't in this case. You solved problems, delegated chores, coalesced into a very effective unit. The bottom line? I believe you have what it takes to be MCOs. Of course, it's not as easy as just saying *sign me up*. There is a rigorous training program, a written test, to get through before you can become a member of Killer Pizza's elite force of monster hunters."

Harvey pulled some files from a desk drawer. He handed a file to each of his employees. "Here is more information on the program. Also included is a contract. Go home. Read through it. Think it over. Do *not* discuss it with parents, siblings, or friends. We insist on complete secrecy here at KP. But by all means, take your time. This is one of the most important decisions you'll make in your life. I don't expect you to be hasty about it."

They simultaneously opened their files. Annabel studied hers for a moment before asking, "Do you always hire people so young, Harvey?"

"Depends on the person. But overall, yes, I do like to hire younger workers. They're enthusiastic. Fast learners. Better than older people at handling the stresses and challenges of this, shall we say, unusual job. Yes, Strobe?"

Strobe was staring intently at Harvey. "Just wondering how old *you* are."

"Twenty-one. Small for my age, I know, but it allows me to pass for a teenager when I go undercover." Harvey smiled, clearly pleased that he had been able to put one over on the trio.

There was a knock on the door, and Steve walked in carrying a large, steaming pizza. "You read my mind,

Steve. Pizza, anyone? Mr. Rogers is still the best in the business at making them."

Toby hungrily accepted a slice of pizza. When he bit into it, he had to admit that Harvey was right about Steve making a great pizza. What was his secret? Did he cook it differently? Did he use a special, unknown ingredient? Toby knew he had to find out. He wanted to make pizzas this good.

Listen to yourself, Toby thought. *There's something called a* guttata *hanging in a refrigerator out there and you're thinking about making pizzas!*

Strobe might have been thinking along similar lines. Chewing on his pizza, he walked out of Harvey's office and headed for the creature. Toby and Annabel joined him. The trio stared solemnly at the bizarre-looking beast.

Harvey watched them from his office doorway. "I think it's only fair to tell you that this guttata was definitely not the only one in the city. Guttata are pack creatures, often with hundreds in a pack. As for our local pack? I believe it is multiplying at a rapid rate."

"Where do these things live?" Strobe asked.

"In nice suburban homes and city apartments, same as you and me. As I told you, they prefer the human form. They're very good at imitating normal, everyday people. But make no mistake, these creatures are a ruthless bunch. They will rigorously defend their turf. I say this as a warning. If you decide to try out for the KP force you'll be getting up close and personal with this fellow's pals very soon. The guttata will do everything they can to find out who took out one of their comrades."

Maybe it was the film they'd just seen. Maybe it was Harvey's revelation of other guttata in the area. But the creature hanging in front of them suddenly looked unnervingly *alive*. It looked as though it might open its eyes at any moment . . .

. . . and glare right at its human audience.

8

When Toby woke the following morning, he lay in bed for a while, thinking about the previous night. Had he really seen what he *thought* he had seen? After tossing that question back and forth for a while, Toby decided . . . no. No way. That thing in Harvey's refrigerator? The monster movie? Had to have been fake. All of it. Or just a bad dream.

Thus convinced, Toby got dressed and went downstairs to get some breakfast. His mother and sister were in the kitchen, his mother making pancakes, his sister sitting at the round, wooden kitchen table. Toby sat down across from Stacey.

"A 'good morning' would be nice," his mother said.

"Good morning," Toby said. He gave his mother a smile as she brought him his pancakes. But then he frowned. Wait . . . what was *that*? Toby stared at his mom as she returned to the counter. Something was going on beneath her blouse. It was as though her body, her skin, was *bubbling*!

Toby heard a grunt from across the table. When he looked at his sister she was eating her pancakes with her hands, stuffing them into her mouth so fast that they were spilling back out. A pancake jam!

What . . . is . . . going . . . on . . . here?!!

Toby looked back at his mom. A growing dread seized his body—pinned him to his chair—as Mrs. Magill slowly turned around to reveal . . . *she now had a guttata face!* The rest of her body quickly followed. Her fingers grew long, pointy talons. Her back hunched up and over, her reptile-like skin bursting through her blouse.

Toby thought he was about to pass out from the shock of what he was seeing. The table suddenly shook, a jolt caused by a temper-tantrum pounding from his sister. Looking at Stacey, Toby saw that she had *transformed into a miniature guttata!* (The change doing nothing to improve her already annoying personality.)

"I want your pancakes!" she said with a fierce snarl. Then she smiled a horrendous smile, bared her long fangs, and leaped across the table at Toby!

■ ■ ■

Toby woke violently.

Then he screamed when he saw his mother standing at the door to his bedroom!

"Toby! What on earth is wrong with you!"

Toby sat up in bed and looked around his bedroom. It was morning. The room was bright and sunny. And his mother . . .

Looked like she normally did.

Whew! Toby thought gratefully. *Just a really bad dream!*

But Toby still had a freak-out hangover from his nightmare. It was, hands down, the most real and unsettling dream he had ever had.

"Honestly. Your face is white as a sheet. Do you feel all right?"

"Uh . . . yeah. I'm okay."

Mrs. Magill studied her son skeptically as Stacey appeared in the hallway behind her. Toby's sister had a devious smirk on her face. She knew her brother was weird. His odd behavior this morning simply served as further evidence of that incontestable fact.

"Show's over, ya little mutant," Toby said.

"Don't speak to your sister like that!"

Stacey grinned and pointed at Toby behind her mom's back. Toby wanted to tackle the brainy brat. Take her right down. Not a good idea, of course. Any disagreement between the two of them, Stacey always won. Thank goodness for easygoing Dad, a reliable buffer between Toby and his stern, disciplinarian mother.

"I just wanted to let you know that someone named Annabel called," Mrs. Magill said, still frowning at Toby. "She said she'd be at Prospect Park at ten o'clock. It's ten till."

Toby jumped out of bed, grabbed a pair of cargo shorts from the floor, pulled them on, slipped on a pair of sandals, and was heading down the stairs before his mom or sister could even react.

"Toby! You need to wash up before leaving this house!"

Toby came back up the stairs, went into the bathroom, and came out with his Polo Sport deodorant. He reached under his T-shirt and slapped on the deodorant as he bounced down the stairs two at a time.

"You can't go out looking like that! Who is this Annabel, anyway?"

"Just someone I work with!"

■ ■ ■

Toby took the shortcut through the woods behind his house to get to Prospect Park. He stopped suddenly when he entered the woods. An eerie quiet permeated the place. No birds. No crickets. No hum of life. Toby was anxious to get to the meeting with Annabel, but something seemed to be drawing him away from the path through the woods, off in the direction where he had seen the mysterious shape after his first day at Killer Pizza.

Walking cautiously along the edge of the woods where it skirted his backyard, inspecting the area as he went, Toby was relieved when he didn't find anything. He was ready to head off when something on the ground caught his eye. There, right between his feet, embedded in an exposed tree root was . . . well, Toby wasn't sure what it was. He knelt, took hold of the object, and pulled. It didn't come out easily, but finally Toby was able to pry the thing loose from the thick root. Holding it up to the light for scrutiny, Toby felt a hot/cold chill.

He was holding a razor-sharp, three-inch-long talon.

Toby had seen a similar talon just the day before. Or rather, *talons*. Did this one belong to the creature currently hanging in Killer Pizza's downstairs refrigerator? Or perhaps one of his guttata pals? Toby wasn't sure, but as he studied the deadly object he felt his flesh crawl. He reached back to throw the talon into the bushes—he just wanted the thing *away* from him—when something made him hesitate. Toby wasn't sure what that "something" was—it was an undefined feeling—but it was enough to cause him to put the talon gingerly into his pocket instead of getting rid of it. With a final look around the strangely quiet woods, Toby headed off to Prospect Park.

■ ■ ■

Prospect Park was not large, but it was nicely situated at the highest point of Hidden Hills and provided an excellent view of the community and the farmland that stretched beyond its borders.

When Toby reached the top of the steps that led to the park—his T-shirt already dark with sweat from the hot, humid day—he saw Strobe and Annabel sitting on the lone park bench by a large maple tree. He waved as he approached his coworkers and sat next to Annabel when he got to the bench. The trio was silent for a moment before Annabel asked, "Get much sleep last night, Toby?"

Toby tried to sound as casual as possible. "Tossed and turned a bit. You?"

"I tossed and turned a *lot*," Annabel replied. "I have to admit, I still have a hard time believing what we saw last night at KP."

That made Toby feel better. Nice to know he wasn't the only one feeling that way.

"So . . . either of you make a decision?" Annabel asked.

"What's to decide?" Strobe said. "I wouldn't miss this for the world. Can't say I'm too happy about the pay, though. Harvey tried to sneak in that little paragraph on the final page of the contract. Minimum wage during our training period? Double minimum wage if we become MCOs? I'm definitely talking to him about that. I expect more than double minimum wage if I'm gonna put my life on the line here."

Toby couldn't believe how cool Strobe was being about all this.

"I was staring up at the ceiling last night when I made my decision," Annabel revealed. "I mean, this is about as far out of the box as you can get, right?" Annabel laughed a short laugh, then frowned. "Actually, it occurred to me that maybe *this* was the reason I was drawn to Killer

Pizza, instead of some other place. Maybe this was simply meant to be for me."

"Don't get all mystical on us, Annabel," Strobe said. "Signing up for Harvey's force is just a job, after all."

"I think you're wrong about that, Strobe. This is about *service*, when you come right down to it. I mean, somebody has to step up and battle these creatures, right?"

"I think you were taken in by that recruiting film, is what I think."

"Maybe I was. One thing's for sure. I'm going in to Killer Pizza as soon as we're done here and giving Harvey my signed contract."

Annabel and Strobe fell silent. Toby was aware that his two partners were silent because they were looking at *him*, waiting to hear what he had decided.

"Uh . . . I don't know, guys. This is all so sudden, you know?"

"It is," Annabel agreed.

"Besides, look at me. Do I look like a monster fighter to you two?" Toby wouldn't have minded if Annabel and Strobe had come back with an immediate "Of course you do!" But instead there was a little hiccup of silence before Annabel said, "Harvey likes us as a team. You have to remember that, Toby. Anyway, we're only signing up for a training period. There's no guarantee we're going to make it."

"You two'll make it. Harvey won't reject you just because I didn't sign up."

"Sounds like you made your decision," Strobe said, standing.

Have I? Toby thought.

Annabel sat next to Toby for a moment, then gave him an encouraging smile. "If you change your mind . . ."

Toby nodded. Strobe headed for the stairs. Annabel gave Toby a final "Sure you don't want to join us?" look, then followed Strobe when Toby stared down at the ground, signaling that he wasn't quite ready to try out to be a Monster Combat Officer.

Watching his coworkers leave the park, Toby felt a sinking sensation in his stomach. Everything had been going so well. Now *this*. He looked at the street below, where a group of kids was playing basketball. It didn't seem right how normal everything looked down there. Toby's world had been turned upside down overnight. Why not everyone else's?

I feel like I've entered the Twilight Zone*!* Toby thought.

Standing to leave, the talon in his pocket gave him a jab, the perfect exclamation point to his *TZ* vibe. Carefully taking out the talon, Toby once again held it up to the light for inspection. As before, a creepy kind of power seemed to emanate from the guttata relic.

And just like that, Toby knew what he had to do. He didn't really want to. He just knew he *had* to. After all, how could he carry on as though nothing had changed in his life?

He couldn't. That's what Toby suddenly realized. He could never go back to being like those kids below, innocently playing basketball on a typical, Hidden Hills July summer morning.

So Toby put the talon back into his cargo shorts pocket and jogged toward the stairs. Strobe and Annabel were almost to the bottom when he called out to them. They stopped and looked back at their partner.

"I'm going with you two." Toby felt powerful and reckless and scared all at the same time when he said those words. He instantly felt like taking them back, but Annabel's smile convinced him otherwise. She looked genuinely pleased to have him on board. So Toby walked down the steps to join his coworkers.

"Okay," Strobe said. "That makes three of us." With

that, Strobe continued down the path that led to the street. Toby hesitated a moment, then followed his two former kitchen colleagues.

And to think only a few weeks ago I was bored! Toby thought as he fell in between Strobe and Annabel and headed off with them down the street, toward Killer Pizza.

PART TWO:
HOW TO BECOME AN MCO

1

"Annabel! Watch out!"

The guttata came at Annabel too quickly. She had no time to set her weapon and fire. The action on the large, curved screen in front of Annabel froze on a snarling close-up of the creature's gnarly face. "Blood" started to drip from the top of the screen.

"GAME OVER."

The lights came on, and Harvey appeared from a booth in the corner. There were three stations in the room—one each for Annabel, Toby, and Strobe—but only one large screen, which allowed them to play the video game simultaneously. A game that Harvey controlled from a computer in his booth.

Harvey did not look happy. *"Watch out?"* he said, glaring at Strobe. "How many times do I have to tell you? It's 'three o'clock'! 'Ten o'clock'! 'Seven'—"

"I know, I know," Strobe said. "I just forgot."

"You *can't* forget! You forget and one of your fellow officers might take a hit. Now let's do it again!"

Harvey strode back to his booth and slammed the door. Strobe gave his boss a cool stare, then settled in with his fellow KP rookies for another round of "Guttata Attack!" A marvel of tech wizardry and electronic sophistication, the simulated battle with the guttata was truly awesome. It blew away anything for sale on the consumer market, that's for sure.

The lights in the room dimmed as the large screen lit up. A group of casually clad, normal-looking men and women appeared on the screen in a suburban, Hidden Hills–type setting. *Then* . . . the suburbanites began to change. Their lifelike, grotesque transformation into a pack of guttata was climaxed by a baring of their fangs. These creatures-from-hell were programmed to do one thing, and one thing only.

Take Toby, Annabel, and Strobe *out*.

■ ■ ■

Two weeks had gone by since Toby, Annabel, and Strobe handed Harvey their signed contracts. Since then, their world had dissolved into a blur of intense study and training.

On the morning of their first official day as rookies in the MCO Academy, Hidden Hills Branch, Harvey had led them on a tour of the secret and surprisingly large basement training center of interconnecting rooms beneath the Killer Pizza building. The tour made it immediately clear where Harvey put most of Killer Pizza's profits.

There was a gym with exercise and bodybuilding machines and a large matted area for self-defense classes. (Taught by Steve Rogers.)

A shooting gallery with pop-up "monster mannequins" for hard target practice. (Harvey in charge.)

The sophisticated computer-game simulation room.

A classroom with an impressive library where Toby, Strobe, and Annabel received instruction from both Harvey and Steve on the monsters that resided—in secret and often among—the human population of the world.

Finally, there was the autopsy and examination room, where the trio had first become aware of the existence of the creature called the guttata.

After the tour, the trio had immediately begun their intense, rigid training schedule, which began at ten A.M. and ended at seven P.M. The schedule was to be repeated every day, six days a week.

In violation of the labor laws for minors, Strobe had pointed out to Harvey.

Harvey countered that normally they would not be training quite so rigorously. But because of the certainty of retaliation from the local guttata pack—not to mention that every day gone by left another innocent person open to infection from their sinister bites—they were on an accelerated crash course.

Toby had the uneasy feeling that Harvey wasn't telling them everything they needed to know about the guttata. Maybe that would come later, in the classroom. In the meantime, there were the workouts and self-defense classes to get through. Toby was already concerned that he might not survive *that* part of his training.

■ ■ ■

"One more! *YOU CAN DO IT!*"

Toby strained at the weight machine as Steve spit in his right ear. His muscles burned! His arms felt like they were going to fall off!

"*DIG!!* I know you have it in you!!!"

Toby was glad Steve knew that, because *he* certainly didn't. Wrestling with an unforgiving metal machine with pulleys and wires and weights had never been his thing. Until two weeks ago, Toby had never worked out a day in his life.

"You're almost there! *ALMOST THERE!!!*"

Toby's muscles gave up trying for "one more." The weights, released from the counterweight of Toby's effort, fell like a shot and hit their base with a loud *CRACK!!!*

Steve stared at Toby, then gave him a reassuring pat on the shoulder. "You'll do it next time," he said casually, his intense drill instructor persona instantly replaced by his normally easygoing personality. Steve turned and walked out of the exercise room.

Toby staggered from the machine, grabbed his towel, and headed for the locker room on rubbery legs. Strobe and Annabel were already there, taking their showers in separate his and her stalls. They always finished their workouts before Toby did.

Strobe's skill in the self-defense classes, his easy mastery of the various weight machines, had come as no surprise to anyone. It was *Annabel* who had caught everyone off guard. Even Harvey, who had noted that Annabel was a quick study, was impressed with her.

The diminutive but agile fourteen-year-old had swiftly become Strobe's almost-equal in the physical part of their training, her lightning quickness allowing her to compete against the much taller Strobe in self-defense class, for example. As for the weight machines, Annabel had tackled them with the same can-do attitude she had shown during Killer Pizza's rocky first week. The bottom line was that Annabel had progressed rapidly and had already established an intense, competitive rivalry with Strobe.

Toby was not happy about how far he was behind his two partners. Even worse, he had no hope of catching up. How could he? For one thing, he was so *tired* all the time. The exhausting pace was already wearing him out. The past two weeks reminded Toby of the time he tried out for the junior high marching band. The hours and hours spent practicing the trombone at home, the after-school practices with the band . . . Toby hadn't been able to handle it, and had quit after a month. And that was just the marching band!

Maybe it would be better, Toby sometimes thought, if he were given his rejection slip right now, instead of at the end of their training. At least that would put him out of his misery.

But every evening, when Toby was home in his bedroom rubbing Icy Hot into his tired, sore muscles, he inevitably opened his desk drawer and took out the talon he had discovered in his backyard. The deadly object never ceased to send a chill up Toby's spine. It was a constant reminder of why he had signed up for KP's MCO Academy in the first place.

MONSTERS TRULY DID EXIST!

If Toby needed a little more inspiration than just the talon, there was always the preface to his *Monsters of the World* textbook. An underground publication whose existence was unknown to anyone other than Killer Pizza MCOs or MCOs-in-training, it was the only text Toby and his partners would be using during their training. The six-hundred-page tome had been written by Harvey's grandfather back in the 1940s and revised and updated by Harvey's father in the 1980s.

The preface to *Monsters of the World* was short, only ten words. But Toby had discovered those ten words had a power to them, not only connecting his training to something larger than just battling guttata, but managing to stir his heart in a way he couldn't quite explain.

The ten words?

"Evil cannot see good, but good can always see evil."

2

Evil was lurking in a city alley, less than ten miles from Toby's house.

The young runaway could sense it somehow. He looked out from inside his large, sturdy cardboard box—home for the night—and studied the alley.

Nothing.

The young man waited for a moment, his eyes scanning the nighttime landscape, just to be sure he wasn't sharing his undesirable piece of downtown real estate with anyone. When he retreated back inside the box, all was quiet. Too quiet, somehow.

CRASH!!!

A large shape suddenly slammed onto the box from above, crumpling it inward. Razor-sharp talons shredded the top of the box and the shape disappeared inside. The young man's screams of alarm were instantly silenced, but the box continued to shudder and split apart from the monster's ferocious attack. Unlike the silent creature that had attacked Chelsea Travers and the kid behind the Echo 8-Plex, this guttata seemed crazed, consumed by bloodlust.

Suddenly, the box was still. After a moment the creature slowly emerged from what was left of the runaway's derelict home. It looked up and down the alley, sniffing. Satisfied there was no more prey in the vicinity, it leaped upward, snatched the lower rung of a fire escape, and crawled quickly to the roof of the warehouse building.

And just like that, all was quiet once again in the alley. Like an afterthought to the horrific attack, a side section of the box that was barely attached to the ravaged structure separated and fell to the ground. Light from the streetlamp at the end of the alley revealed there was nothing left inside. Not even a shoe. Or a shred of clothing. The guttata had been very thorough. Or hungry.

Either way, on this night . . . evil had feasted.

3

WHOOOOSH!!!!

THUNK!

The steel arrow with the titanium tip slammed into the guttata mannequin's heart. Toby exhaled with relief. After almost three weeks of trying, he'd finally hit a bull's-eye!

"Excellent, Toby!" Annabel gave him a high five as Harvey walked from behind the shooting counter and looked at his three rookies.

"What's the matter, chief?" Strobe asked. "You look kinda bummed. Aren't we comin' along fast enough for you?"

Harvey didn't answer right away, which made Toby uneasy. In spite of his bull's-eye, *he* wasn't the one coming along fast enough.

"Steve and I got word of an incident downtown last night," Harvey revealed.

"What happened?" Annabel asked.

"If you asked the police that question, they'd say no comment. That's because they have no idea what happened. The only thing they have to go on is a bloody box."

"Guttata?" Strobe asked.

"That's my guess. This victim wasn't being recruited, however."

Toby felt his stomach do a little somersault at this news. He had read about the guttata's occasional zombie-like urges in *Monsters of the World*. Was that the case here?

"So, you think . . ." Annabel began.

"The victim was eaten. Yes."

Harvey's disgusting news had a predictable sobering effect on the trio's mood.

"This doesn't change anything," Harvey said. "We continue to train and study just as hard as we have been."

"I couldn't agree more," Strobe said. "But I do have a suggestion. I think we need to start in with these babies." Strobe was referring to an impressive array of high-tech guns and rifles that hung on a nearby wall.

"All in due time, Strobe. For now, we will continue to concentrate on the crossbow. It's actually the best for

suburban combat, which is what we'll mainly be involved with. The less noise in this environment the better. Besides, when used properly, the crossbow is just as
effective as any of these other weapons."

Eying the hardware on the wall, Strobe looked disappointed that he wouldn't be getting his hands on
them any time soon. As for Toby, he liked his crossbow.
Designed by Harvey, it was an ingenious high-tech variation on an ancient weapon. Lightweight but strong as
steel, the collapsible KP weapon was fitted with a mul-
tiple arrow cartridge and was deadly accurate, thanks
to a high-powered viewfinder and laser-tracker beam.

"It is time to add a new wrinkle to your crossbow
practice, however." Harvey indicated two large doors
behind the trio. "Annabel, would you open those cabi-
net doors, please?"

The trio was impressed with what they saw inside.
There were racks of black, ultrathin chest plates; forearm, bicep, and leg plates; dark-tinted NVGs (night
vision goggles); and backpacks of various sizes.

"Find the armor that fits you best," Harvey instructed. "A pair of goggles that feel comfortable. Select
a backpack. From now on, you will be conducting target practice in this gear."

Strobe was the first to strap a chest plate on over his T-shirt. It gave him the cool look of a Roman warrior. Annabel and Toby were right behind him. After the trio finished suiting up and snapped an extra arrow cartridge into the receiving lock on their bicep plate, Harvey gave them a once-over, then said, "First one to hit three bull's-eyes in their armor gets a break from this afternoon's workout."

Annabel and Strobe quickly tied each other with two bull's-eyes. But Strobe proved to be faster on the draw, faster at getting his extra arrow cartridge from bicep plate clip to crossbow, and won the competition.

■ ■ ■

"Come with me, please."

Sitting at their desks in the classroom, Toby, Annabel, and Strobe exchanged perplexed looks, then followed Harvey out into the hallway. They were supposed to have their first test, covering the exhaustive chapters on the guttata, but from the looks of it, they were going to be spared that ordeal.

On the way up the spiral staircase, Harvey explained that Killer Pizza's deliveryman had just walked off the job. With Steve off in New York to deal with a nasty outbreak of mind-altering parasites in the Tribeca area,

Harvey was the only one at the shop with a driver's license, thus the only one legally able to deliver one large Fangtastic Hawaiian, several orders of Beasties, and one Monstrosity to a birthday party at a nearby Hidden Hills home.

"Why are we going with you?" Strobe asked.

Harvey didn't answer Strobe's question. He simply led the trio through the kitchen and out to the official Killer Pizza red-and-black MINI Cooper delivery car.

■ ■ ■

"As I mentioned the other day," Harvey said, turning onto Hazel Street from Industrial Avenue, "forensic testing has indicated that the guttata I eliminated had two different types of human blood in its system when it died. There were no human remains in its stomach, so these victims were definitely recruits. Strobe, what kind of symptoms might the two guttata victims be experiencing right about now?"

Aha. The trio wasn't getting out of the test, after all. It had simply become an oral test.

"Uhhhhh . . . let me think. . . ." Strobe said.

Harvey waited a few seconds, then said, "Toby? Symptoms from a guttata bite?"

"Fever, fatigue, weight loss, possible hallucinations . . ."

"Annabel?"

"Gastrointestinal discomfort, heart palpitations. Most significantly, a shaking of the left hand."

"Correct. Strobe, what are some characteristics of a guttata pack?"

Once again, Strobe was at a loss for words.

"Annabel?"

"They're ruled by an Alpha Male. The Alpha is a pure, direct descendant of the original guttata. They're the only guttata that have wings. They can live for more than three hundred years."

"Good. Toby, other characteristics of a guttata pack?"

"Well, they have this weird monthly ritual held on the night of the new moon called the Gathering. The guttata gather to drink a lifesaving secretion spit out by their Alpha Male."

Strobe smiled at Toby's answer, his expression suggesting that he was hearing this information for the first time. Harvey shot him a look in his rearview mirror. "Did you study for the quiz, Strobe?"

"Well . . . not really. I'm pretty tired at night."

"So is everyone else. Let me tell you something. You may be the best at physical combat, but without the knowledge to go along with your physical skills, you will not graduate from this program. Understand?"

Strobe was silent.

"*Strobe*. Do you understand?"

Strobe finally gave Harvey a grudging nod.

"The written test will be tomorrow. This was just a warm-up." Harvey turned onto a street near North Park, the large, sprawling haven of green where Chelsea Travers had met her fate. "I confronted the guttata on the far side of this park. Which means its victims might be somewhere in this vicinity. I want all of you to be on the lookout for anyone displaying symptoms of a guttata bite. It's like finding a needle in a haystack, I realize, but you never know."

"Can you do anything for these two if we find them?" Annabel asked.

"I do have an antidote for my MCOs if they're bitten during combat. But for these two, I'm afraid too much time has already passed. If we find them, at least we'll be able to prevent them from being indoctrinated into the local pack after their transformation."

"I've been wondering something, Harvey," Toby said. "Is there any way to tell if a human is a guttata? I mean, how do we track these monsters down? I haven't read anything about that in the text."

"That's the rub," Harvey replied. "As I told you, guttata blend into their communities very well. *Too* well. That's why Steve and I are trying to locate the Alpha Male. If we eliminate him, we eliminate the pack. Toby, would you please tell Strobe why that is?"

Toby didn't like Strobe being put on the spot like this, but his boss had just asked him a question, so he figured he should answer it. "The pack needs this life-saving spit from the Alpha Male, so they're toast if they don't get it."

"Correct. If we can take out the Alpha, his pack will have to leave the city, try to find a new Alpha. They'll die within a few months, the younger ones even sooner, if they can't locate a new pack. Which is what we're hoping for. Guttata are still pretty scarce on this continent. We want to keep it that way."

"So lemme at the big guy," Strobe said.

"You're not ready for an Alpha, Strobe," Harvey said. "Just to give you an idea, the guttata I eliminated is a pup by comparison."

Yikes! Toby thought. *I think I prefer the ones in the shooting gallery!*

Harvey pulled up to the curb in front of a large, two-story house. Purple, green, and black balloons—each one featuring a classic, scowling monster's face—were tied to the mailbox and the railing around the front porch. It was a monster-themed birthday party!

"Here we are," Harvey said. "Strobe, why don't you do the honors?"

Strobe shot Harvey a look as Annabel handed him four pizza sleeves from the front seat.

"Punishment for not studying for the test?"

"Look on the bright side. You get to keep the tip."

Strobe got out and walked toward the house. A couple of six-year-olds bounded out the front door and grabbed at the pizza sleeves as Strobe stepped onto the porch.

"Killer Pizza's here!" one of them yelled.

"Keep your grubby hands off the merchandise!" Strobe ordered.

Harvey shook his head at the sight of Strobe brushing past the hungry, hyper kids. "Good way to represent Killer Pizza, Strobe."

Toby smiled when even more kids piled out of the house. He couldn't wait to see how Strobe was going to handle *them*. But his attention was suddenly drawn to a first-floor window in the house. A woman was standing at the window, staring outside. Her expression was not what you'd expect, considering the festive event going on in the house. The woman looked . . . blank, really. Her face was drained of any emotion.

Toby felt a chill run through his body as he stared at the woman. Much like the night when he heard the strange howl on his way home from Killer Pizza, or when he found the talon in the woods behind his house, Toby felt as though he was in the presence of something . . . not good.

That woman's not a guttata! Toby told himself.

Actually, why not? Toby wouldn't be able to tell even if she was. Anyone on the *street* could be a guttata, for that matter. The kid mowing the lawn a few houses away. The two women talking on a nearby front porch. The FedEx guy who—come to think of it—had given Toby a pretty strange look when they drove past his truck.

You're just being paranoid, Toby tried to convince himself. But then . . .

POP!!!

Toby jerked violently when he heard the explosion. He whipped around to see that it was one of the balloons that had caused the sound. Bursting in the noontime sun, the tattered remains were floating listlessly to the ground. His heart racing, Toby stared at the pulverized balloon, then had to laugh at how ridiculously tense he was.

"You okay, Toby?" Annabel was looking over the front seat at him.

"Yeah, sure."

As if to convince himself, Toby glanced back at the balloon. Yeah, that's what had caused the sound that had given him a mini heart attack.

As for the woman in the window?

When Toby looked at the house, she was no longer there.

4

A large two-story building reflected in dark sun-
glasses. The man wearing the glasses tipped his hat to
an older woman as he arrived at the entrance to the
building and held the door open for her to enter in front
of him.

"Thank you, Officer," the woman said with a smile.

"You're welcome." The man's voice carried an edgy
authority. Entering the air-conditioned building, he took
off his sunglasses, his police hat, and wiped his bald
head with a handkerchief. The people in the building
nodded and said hello to him as he passed. They all
knew him and treated him with careful respect. That's
because the man was second-in-command of the Brentwood Hills Police Department, a community that bordered one side of Hidden Hills.

What no one in the building could have suspected
was that the man was also a guttata.

Not just *any* guttata, however. Thomas Gome had been given the responsibility of tracking down the people responsible for taking out one of the pack's more prominent members. (The guttatas' Alpha leader was assuming the worst, that their missing comrade was dead.)

As Gome approached his office, a woman sitting behind a nearby desk pulled a file from a desk drawer. "The missing persons report you requested, Mr. Gome."

Gome nodded, took the file, and entered his office. The blinds were closed against the harsh afternoon sun. No lights were on. In the darkness it would be easy to miss the silent figure sitting in the chair in the corner of the room. A match suddenly flared, illuminating a pair of intensely luminous blue eyes. Dressed totally in black, the woman with the stylishly punked-out hair lit her cigarette, inhaled, and blew out a cloud of smoke, all the while staring coolly at Gome.

The policeman tossed the missing persons file onto the woman's lap. She was here because she had been chosen to track down the missing guttata's "marks" and bring them into the pack. It was an important job, one that would overlap Gome's work.

Gome and the blue-eyed woman were aware it might take a while to complete their assignments. The missing guttata had not revealed to anyone where he was going to troll for marks on the day that he disappeared. It could have been anywhere in the city. That was a lot of ground to cover.

But these two were confident they would not fail their Alpha leader. The guttata "recruits" would be found and brought into the pack. The people who had brought harm to their colleague would be tracked down and dealt with in the appropriate manner. "Appropriate" in this case meaning . . . liquidation.

Guttata-style.

5

Toby was in his bedroom—door firmly closed to prevent unwelcome visitors—watching an episode of his favorite female chef's cooking show. He had downloaded the show on his computer a few weeks before but hadn't had any time to watch it.

After getting home from KP that afternoon, Toby decided to *give* himself the time. It was clear to him that he needed a break from all things guttata, at least for one evening. No studying. No worrying about whether or not any of those monsters lived on his street. Or whether or not he was even going to graduate from the KP program. It was time to shut down the weirdness, even for a few hours, and do something normal for a change.

Toby definitely felt better as he watched the hostess of *At Home in Italy* move about her beautifully stocked kitchen, instructing the uninformed masses how to properly prepare Pizza Rustica.

"Four ounces thinly sliced prosciutto, coarsely chopped, one quarter cup grated Pecorino Romano, two teaspoons minced garlic, one half slightly beaten egg . . ." Toby dutifully wrote down the recipe in his private cuisine notebook, which he kept hidden in a desk drawer, right next to *Monsters of the World*.

Before the program was over, however, Toby felt his eyes droop. His first evening off in almost three weeks, and he couldn't even make it through a half-hour program!

Frustrating.

Just go to bed, Toby told himself. *Sleep for twelve straight hours and you'll feel better in the morning.*

But the thought of calling it a night and going to bed so early didn't appeal to Toby. So, what to do? It didn't take long for Toby to come up with an answer. He went downstairs, told his parents he was going out for a bit, hopped on his bike, and took off for the Hidden Hills Fun Zone.

"The Zone" featured an indoor video arcade and an outdoor miniature golf course and batting cages. It was always crawling with kids—especially in the summer—and Toby felt instantly energized as he approached the entertainment complex. Zipping around a group of Triple H kids, he rode up to the bike rack, secured his GT Palomar, and went into the arcade, where he bought a hot dog at the Dog Zone.

Leaning up against the counter, Toby looked out across the huge playtime palace. Yeah, this was more like it. Havin' a dog, checkin' out the video arcade to see what's shakin'. Toby had spent a ton of time in the place when he was eleven, twelve years old, so he felt right at home. But he had forgotten just how *deafening* the place was.

He had also forgotten what a Dog Zone hot dog tasted like. Taking a bite, Toby had to stifle an impulse to spit the mouthful right back out onto the floor. It was terrible!

"Hey, Seth," Toby said, turning back to the fourteen-year-old who was behind the hot dog counter. "You should think about putting out some different kinds of condiments for these dogs. Something interesting, maybe a cilantro, roasted pecan dip. Or a Mexican bean kind of thing. Hey, how about fennel? That has a licorice kind of flavor. That'd be different, worth trying." Toby got excited, just thinking about the mouthwatering seasoning variations.

Seth looked at Toby blankly, as if the endless noise in the arcade had zapped his brain to the point of coma. Toby gave an understanding nod to Seth, then headed off into the maze of video machines, tossing his hot dog into a nearby trash can as he went.

I could show these people how to improve the Dog Zone!

Toby had to smile when he realized what that said about how much he missed being in the Killer Pizza kitchen. He was coming up with ideas on how to improve a hot dog!

The fact was, Toby really did miss being in the KP kitchen. In addition to his hyper/exhausted state, that had been one of the really negative side effects of signing up for the KP academy. Just when Toby had felt like he was beginning to get better and more comfortable as a pizza chef, "Doug" had revealed himself to be Harvey.

"Tubby! I mean, Toby. What's happenin'?" Toby felt someone grab him on the shoulder. "Whoa! Check it out. Aliens take over your body or something? You're kinda *toned* there, man."

The happy grabber was Jordan Marley, a classmate of Toby's at Hidden Hills Middle School. The two usually sat close to each other because of their last names. Magill and Marley. It had been that way since grade school. Toby didn't like sitting near Jordan. He was a coarse, physical kind of kid.

"Yeah, Jordan, aliens took over my body," Toby said, eying the arcade exit. He was pleased that Jordan had noticed his improved physique—so had his dad the other day, Toby's slightly slimmer, more muscular body being one of the *positive* side effects of signing up for the KP academy—but that didn't mean he wanted to hang out with the guy.

"What's up with that?" Jordan said. "Gonna try out for football in the fall?"

"No, don't think so."

"You should. You'd be good on the line. Hey, I'm off to take on Monster Menace. Wanna play?"

"Thanks, but I'm gonna do a round of golf."

"See ya!"

Jordan disappeared into the crowd. Toby watched him go with a shake of his head, then went outside. The stale air in the arcade was already getting to him.

Toby felt better when he hit the golf course. Tapping a small, colored golf ball down the worn green runways of the Fun Zone golf course had always made Toby feel . . . happy. Maybe it was how simple the game was. Put the ball in the hole. That was it. Uncomplicated. As opposed to life, which was seldom as simple. Especially lately.

Toby had happily played six holes and was waiting to start the seventh hole when he saw the girl with the trembling left hand. That changed Toby's fun evening in a shot, his posture going rigid as adrenaline exploded through his body.

The girl was with Lenny and his crew, who were playing a few holes in front of Toby. When the girl turned to get a drink of water from a nearby fountain Toby was shocked to see that it was Chelsea Travers.

Yes, Chelsea.

It had been more than a month since a young couple had discovered her around one o'clock in the morning, still lying in the middle of the road near North Park. Chelsea had no memory of being rescued, just the part where she came to in the emergency room of a local hospital. She had immediately made the mistake of telling the emergency room doctor that she was bitten by some sort of strange creature.

Say it again? The bite on Chelsea's thigh was real enough, but a strange creature?

Chelsea quickly learned not to mention that ever again. Not to the other doctors her father had taken her to see over the past few weeks. Not to Lenny and her friends. Fact was, at this point Chelsea wasn't sure *what* she had seen that night. All she was certain of was that she felt absolutely terrible.

Toby knew Chelsea only by sight. He'd never talked to her. She was a year older than he was, but everyone knew Chelsea because she was the notorious Lenny Baker's girlfriend.

Right now Toby wasn't concerned about who Chelsea dated. What worried him was how she looked. She'd lost so much weight since the last time he had seen her! Before he knew what he was doing, Toby was on his way toward Chelsea, his heart beating faster the closer he got to her. Harvey hadn't told the trio what to do after spotting a possible victim of a guttata bite. But Toby knew he had to do *something*. After all . . .

Weight loss. A pallor to the skin. A trembling *left* hand. Chelsea had three of the telltale symptoms.

"Hi, Chelsea."

Chelsea turned around slowly from the drinking fountain when she heard Toby's greeting. She looked right at Toby, but her eyes were glazed, unfocused.

"You probably don't know me, but my name's Toby Magill."

"Yeah?" Chelsea said.

Toby hesitated. Okay. Here he was. Now what? He couldn't launch into a lecture on guttata, that's for sure.

"I have a question for you, Chelsea. I know this might sound weird, but . . . were you bitten by anything the past few months?"

The look Chelsea gave Toby was suddenly animated with so many emotions, emotions that seemed to flit across the surface of her eyes. Fear. Denial. Resignation. But hope, maybe, as well?

Before Chelsea could answer Toby's question, someone gripped him painfully on the arm and spun him around. Toby groaned inwardly before he even saw who had twirled him around like a top. He *knew* who it was.

Lenny Baker.

Shaved head, heavily muscled, Baker was the kind of person you just didn't want to cross. The "king bully" of Hidden Hills High was legendary in the area. The guy seemed to have a sixth sense for zeroing in on a person's weakness and attacking, either verbally or physically. Often both.

"What do you think you're doin'?" Lenny said, his sharp, angry eyes promising violence, very soon. "Hittin' on my girl?"

"No, of course not. I was just . . ."

"It's okay, Lenny," Chelsea said.

"It's *not* okay! I don't like dudes who think they can just walk up to my girl and start talking to her!" Lenny hit Toby in the chest with a short, powerful punch. Stumbling backward, his arms whirling comically, Toby barely managed to stay upright.

"Sorry. I won't do it again," Toby gasped when he was able to catch his breath, which Lenny's punch had knocked right out of him.

"Sorry's not good enough, dude." Lenny grabbed Toby by the front of his T-shirt. *Oh, boy, here it comes,* Toby thought. *I'm gonna be eatin' my front teeth in about two seconds!*

"You don't let him go, you'll find your lower cheeks parked in the thirteenth-hole pond."

Lenny's cocked fist froze by his right ear. Still holding Toby by the T-shirt, he turned his head slowly to see Strobe standing behind him. Lenny smiled, let Toby go, and squared off with Strobe.

"And who's gonna do that?" Lenny asked.

"I'll be more than happy to," Strobe replied.

Toby made no move to stop what looked like an inevitable clash between the two. For one thing, he was too fascinated by what he was seeing. This was the type of thing he'd only seen in the movies!

Lenny's friends quickly gathered behind him, pushing Toby out of the way. "Looks like you might have your hands full," Lenny said.

Strobe didn't blink. "I can handle it."

Lenny laughed. "Think so?" Lenny's icy smile disappeared as quickly as it had appeared. "Give it your best shot. . . ."

"Break it up!" A beefy, bullnecked security guard pushed his way through the crowd that had started to cluster around Toby, Strobe, and Lenny. "You *hear* me?!" the guard demanded.

Like air seeping out of a balloon, the tension that had instantly gripped the crowd ("Check it out! A *fight*!") started to dissipate. Lenny and Company looked cheated. They really *wanted* this, if for no other reason than to break up the boredom of another long summer evening.

"Hand over the putters!" the guard ordered. Lenny's crew, holding putters in one hand and different-colored golf balls in the other, suddenly looked very silly.

"We paid for a round of golf," one of them yelled belligerently.

"*Tough!* Hand them over!"

There was a moment of hesitation, as though Lenny and his pals were not going to comply with the guard's ultimatum. Then, mumbling and cursing among themselves, they filed slowly past the guard, handing over their putters and balls as they went. Lenny gave Strobe a hard bump when he followed his crew out of the Fun Zone golf course. "See ya around sometime."

Cool as could be, Strobe just smiled. Chelsea was right behind Lenny. As she passed Toby she gave him a glance. Toby wanted to grab her. Take her with him. But he knew he had to find another way to help her. He'd call *Harvey*. That's what he'd do.

"You two, as well." The guard positioned himself in front of Strobe and Toby, as though he expected them to make a dash for the video arcade. "C'mon. *Out*."

Strobe turned and started for the exit. Toby fell in silently next to him. He felt completely drained all of a sudden. And ashamed that he hadn't made a move to face down Lenny's gang with Strobe.

How do you expect to do battle with a pack of guttata if you can't face down a group of high school punks? Toby thought, thoroughly disappointed in himself.

"See you tomorrow," Strobe said, heading off when they had arrived at the parking lot.

"Hey, where you going?"

"Home."

"How'd you get here, walk?"

Strobe nodded.

"Want a ride on my bike?"

Strobe smiled. "Don't think so."

"Yeah, right. That wouldn't be too cool, would it?"

Strobe waved as he walked off. It wasn't until Toby got to his bike that he realized he hadn't thanked Strobe for saving his butt.

6

"Chelsea never went home last night."

Toby sank dejectedly into the chair facing Harvey's desk. The news his boss had just given him was like a punch to the gut.

"I should have never let her out of my sight."

What Toby *had* done was call Harvey right after Strobe had walked off into the night. Harvey had told Toby to go on home. He and Steve would deal with it.

"Don't beat yourself up about this," Harvey said. "You did the right thing. How could you have known what Chelsea would do? Or *wouldn't* do? Besides, it would have been kind of difficult following her car on your bike, don't you think?"

Good point. But Toby still felt bad. No, terrible. He couldn't get the image of Chelsea's searching look—the look she'd given him after he'd asked her if she had been bitten by anything—out of his head. She had looked so . . . vulnerable. And scared.

"So what do we do?" Toby asked. "Form a search party?"

"Yes. But not until this evening. If Chelsea has gone off to begin her transformation, there's no way we'll be able to track her down during the day. At night, she might be out and about, looking for food."

Picturing Chelsea—probably out in the woods somewhere—beginning her otherworldly transformation made Toby feel sick. Literally. He felt like he might upchuck his breakfast.

"There's nothing you can do right now," Harvey insisted. "Best to keep busy."

Toby knew that meant he should get back to his training. He sat silently for a moment, then pushed himself up from his chair and walked out of the office.

■ ■ ■

"No! It goes in like *this*!" Annabel was obviously annoyed with Strobe as she showed him how to quickly collapse his crossbow and properly insert it into his MP (Monster Patrol) backpack.

The trio's assignment for the day was repeatedly assembling and collapsing their crossbows as quickly as possible. In addition, they were to don their MP gear until they could do it with their eyes closed. At the end of the day, Harvey was going to test them.

Annabel and Strobe stopped what they were doing when Toby came into the gym. "Chelsea never went home," Toby said in answer to their questioning looks. "We're going out to look for her tonight."

"Why not today?" Annabel asked. "Why not right now?"

"She's probably in hiding during the day, Harvey said."

Annabel angrily brushed past Toby on her way out of the gym, obviously on her way to talk to Harvey. Toby looked at Strobe. "What's wrong with Annabel?"

"Nothin'."

"What do you mean, nothin'? I've never seen her like this. Were you giving her a hard time about something?"

"Hey, check it out. Toby protecting his girl."

"She's not my girl. I just know how you can be sometimes, Strobe."

Strobe shrugged, then shoved a long, gleaming knife into the sheath on his forearm plate. "Maybe I have been a little testy today. I'm tired of all this training, is what it is. Let's get on with it, you know? Time to look these monster goons in the eye. Time for some action."

"We've been doing this less than a month."

"That's enough for me."

Toby didn't doubt it was enough time for Strobe. Not after last night. Strobe was the kind of guy you wanted in the trenches with you, that's for sure.

Toby found himself thinking about the events of the previous night as he arranged his gear in preparation for a run-through. "So, anyway . . . thanks for helping me out at The Zone last night."

Strobe nodded. That was the extent of his response. Just a cool nod.

"What were you doing there, anyway?" Strobe didn't strike Toby as the type of guy who would go in for a place like The Zone.

"Batting cage."

"Batting cage? You play baseball?"

"No. I just like to whack a ball as hard as I can every now and then."

Toby nodded. Ooookay. "By the way, do you go to Triple H, Strobe?"

"I will in the fall. I just moved here."

"Yeah? When?"

"Just before I got the job at Killer Pizza."

"Where were you living before?"

"No offense, Toby, but last night doesn't mean you can interview me like a talk show host."

Toby *was* offended by Strobe's brush-off. He thought that maybe something had changed in their relationship because of the incident the previous night. Obviously, Strobe didn't feel that way. Fine, if that's the way Strobe wanted it, Toby figured he'd just leave him be. It felt like too much of an effort trying to connect with the guy.

Toby was halfway through putting on his body armor when Annabel came back into the room.

"Talk Harvey into going out to look for Chelsea before nightfall?" Strobe asked.

"We don't have to look for her. She's upstairs."

"What?" Toby said, shocked. "What's she doing here?"

"She wants to talk to you, Toby."

Toby couldn't believe it. "Does Harvey know that?"

Annabel nodded. "He said you should go up alone, first. She might get suspicious otherwise. Just be cool, Harvey said. Like you have no idea what she wants to talk to you about."

Toby was almost out of the room when Annabel said, "Uh . . . Toby?"

"Yeah?"

"Don't you think you should take off your armor?"

"Oh . . . right."

Chelsea was waiting for Toby outside Killer Pizza. Pacing back and forth on the sidewalk, she looked extremely agitated. Toby tried on what he hoped came across as a casual smile as he pushed through the front door. "Hi, Chelsea. How'd you know this is where I worked?"

Turning at the sound of Toby's voice, Chelsea gave Toby an inscrutable look behind her dark sunglasses. "You were wearing a Killer Pizza hat last night. It seemed like a good place to start." In the unforgiving light of the afternoon sun Chelsea looked worse than she had the night before. Her face was beaded with sweat and her tank top was soaked clear through. She looked like she'd just gone swimming in her clothes.

"C'mon inside," Toby said, opening the door.

"I'd rather not." Chelsea shot a skittish look over her shoulder, as though she was worried that someone had followed her to Killer Pizza.

"Chelsea," Toby said softly, dispensing with any attempt to appear cool, calm, and collected. "Please." He stood at the door, holding it open for Chelsea. "There's an office we can go to. It's private."

Chelsea thought about that, then walked through the

111

door. Toby led her past the reception area, through the kitchen, and down the hall to Steve's office. He quickly pulled the only chair in the room out from behind Steve's desk and offered it to Chelsea. She sank into it gratefully.

"Can I get you something to drink?"

"A Pepsi would be great."

"How about a glass of water?" Toby thought that might be better for some reason.

"I need the caffeine." Chelsea had been *living* on caffeine the past few weeks.

"I'll get you both."

Toby ran down the hall, quickly filled two glasses, and hurried back to Steve's office. He didn't want to give Chelsea any time to change her mind about being at Killer Pizza. She had that look about her—like a scared animal. Like she could bolt at any second. Toby certainly didn't want to lose her a second time.

But when Toby entered the office, Chelsea was gone! A brief moment of panic, then Toby realized that Chelsea had not left the room. She was behind the desk, making an alarmingly odd gagging kind of sound.

Toby quickly put down the Pepsi and water and hurried around the desk. What greeted him was the horrifying sight of Chelsea convulsing, her hands clenched like claws, her body racked with spasms. As dismaying as it was to see Chelsea in such a state, it was her *skin* that had stopped Toby right in his tracks. It had turned dark and light, irregularly spotted. A gruesome sight if there ever was one. Chelsea now had the distinctive-looking skin of a guttata!

Toby stood stock-still for a moment, then charged out of the office to get Harvey.

7

Intense movement and energy in the classroom.

Harvey and Steve had quickly transformed the room into a mini-hospital, producing a hospital bed, IVs, and monitors. It all looked very professional. Like the real deal.

Where'd all this stuff come from? Toby wondered as he watched Harvey and Steve place Chelsea on the bed. Harvey had given Chelsea a shot as soon as he got to the office, which had put her right out. But even though Chelsea was unconscious from the sedative, her body was not relaxed. It was as though she had frozen in the midst of one of her convulsions. Not a pretty sight.

The classroom was weirdly appropriate for this paramedic operation. Hanging on the walls were dozens of pictures of weird and fantastic monsters. Sharing wall space with the fiends were blueprint drawings of the numerous KP weapons used to fight the creatures of the night.

But the really eerie thing about Chelsea being in the classroom was "Sammy." That was the name Strobe had bestowed on the guttata from the refrigerator, the actual creature that had infected Chelsea with its bite. The beast had been autopsied and was now on display in front of the blackboard, a speckled, otherworldly variation on the classroom skeleton.

"Toby!" Harvey said, snapping him out of his strangely detached, light-headed daze. Harvey tossed Toby something that looked like an armband. "Put that around Chelsea's left bicep and plug it in there." Harvey pointed to a monitor set up near the head of the bed.

Strobe suddenly burst through the door, pushing a cart overflowing with bags of ice.

"Good," Harvey said. "Leave the ice in the bags. Pack 'em around Chelsea's body."

As Strobe, Steve, and Annabel concentrated on that task, Toby lifted Chelsea's frail arm to put on the armband. "Shouldn't we take her to the hospital?" he asked.

"They wouldn't know what to do with her," Harvey replied as he inserted a needle into a vein in Chelsea's right arm. "Probably kill her trying to save her."

"But I thought you said it was doubtful you could do anything for someone who was bitten by a guttata."

"I have to *try*, at least, don't I?" Harvey snapped.

Toby figured he'd better stop with the questions. When he had plugged the armband into the monitor, he stood back from the action.

"Okay, good," Harvey said after everyone was done with their tasks. "Annabel? Keep a watch on the ice. You'll probably have to replace it every half hour or so, initially. We need to get her temperature down, and fast." The monitor, which digitally revealed Chelsea's temperature, currently read 105 degrees.

"I'll be in to check on her regularly, but let me know immediately if there's any change. Strobe and Toby? I want you to continue with your training. After an hour, one of you can relieve Annabel so she can get her practice in. Any questions?"

Toby couldn't believe it. Harvey still wanted them to *train*? How could he concentrate on that while Chelsea was lying here in such a state? But he didn't ask those questions out loud. After Harvey had left the room, Steve—always more sensitive than his boss—gave Toby a pat on the shoulder. "We're doing all we can right now," he said.

Even after the trio had finished their training for the day they continued to help look after Chelsea. By nightfall her temperature was down to 101 degrees, an encouraging sign. Plus, her body had finally relaxed, and her skin, although still visibly guttata-like, was returning to normal.

Chelsea was not out of the danger zone, however. Not even close. For one thing, her metabolism was still "completely haywire," as Harvey put it in layman's terms.

"Go home," Harvey told them as they all sat in the classroom, sharing a couple of pizzas Steve had prepared for them. "Steve and I will watch her tonight."

Toby didn't want to leave Chelsea. He felt like she was his responsibility, somehow. He was about to tell Harvey that he wanted to stay longer when Steve appeared at the door. "Harvey? We have visitors."

Toby's first thought was that Chelsea's parents had arrived. Maybe Harvey had called them to explain about their daughter. Or maybe it was the police. They were certainly out looking for Chelsea by now.

"Guttata."

Wait. . . . What did Steve just say?

Harvey stood and calmly tossed the rest of his pizza into the trash can. He had asked Steve to go on patrol in the general area, concerned that Chelsea may have attracted some of their local "otherworldlies."

"Where are they?" Harvey asked.

"East. That wooded area near Turtle Creek."

"Headed this way?"

"Could be. But they might be up to something a little more sinister than just trying to track us down."

What could be more sinister than a group of guttata coming to get us? Toby wondered.

"I heard over the local police frequency that a Hidden Hills boy has gone missing," Steve explained as if in response to Toby's thought.

"If that's the case, there's no time to lose," Harvey said. He looked at his three rookies. "Shall we?"

"Are you kidding?" Strobe asked. "Are we really off to fight these guys?"

"If we have to."

"All right! What about Chelsea?" Toby asked.

"I'll be staying with her," Steve said.

"You look a little freaked, man," Strobe said. "Maybe you should stay, too."

That ticked Toby off. Strobe didn't think he was ready

to fight the guttata? He gulped down the rest of his pizza slice and stood up from his classroom chair. "Let's go," he managed to mumble around the pizza with as much bravado as he could manage. A slow smile spread across Strobe's face at Toby's response.

Harvey nodded at his team, then led the way out of the room.

Strobe gave Sammy a quick right jab as he followed Harvey. The short punch caused the hideous classroom specimen to sway back and forth. It looked like a bizarre pendulum, ticking off the moments until Toby, Strobe, and Annabel would face their first real test.

This isn't practice anymore, Toby thought with a jolt as he passed the swinging guttata. It wasn't a game. Ready or not . . .

. . . this was "do or die" time.

8

There were six guttata. They were in human form.
They were at the bottom of a steep ravine in a heavily
wooded area.

Harvey had tracked the guttata to this very spot, using a self-designed radar device that homed in on the
ultrahigh body temperature of a wide range of creatures. He and his three rookies now watched from their
hiding place in the woods as the guttata piled branches
onto a fire that blazed in the middle of a small clearing.

Toby felt like a commando fighter, lying in the underbrush as he watched the creepy figures through his
NVGs. A very *nervous* commando fighter. The black-clad
group was no less intimidating in human form, that's for
sure. Moving back and forth among the trees, stoking the
fire, they gave off an intensely scary vibe. They looked
like they were conducting some kind of tribal ritual.

"Is that what I think it is, lying on the ground?" Annabel whispered. She was referring to a motionless form near the fire.

"It's a young boy, all right," Harvey confirmed, squinting through his night vision telescope.

"Is he dead?" Annabel asked.

"No. Unconscious."

"What are these freaks doing?" Strobe asked. "Initiating the poor dude into the pack?"

"He looks too young for that. This one they probably just want to gobble down. These guttata don't look much older than you guys. Which is good. That'll make them easier to deal with than the older, more experienced guttata. They'll still put up a nasty fight, believe me, but if we can take 'em by surprise, it'll confuse them, prevent them from turning guttata. At least for a bit."

Toby hadn't heard the last part of what Harvey said. He was too grossed out by the first part. It was one thing to read about the guttata's unsavory eating habits, but no way did Toby want to witness such a horrifying sight. Especially for the kid's sake.

"I'm going to the other side," Harvey whispered. "Strobe, go left. Annabel, right. Toby, you stay right here.

Take aim at the guttata nearest you. When you hear my whistle, fire. Got it?"

Before Toby knew it, he was alone in the woods. He could feel his pulse throbbing through his neck veins, his heart was beating so fast.

I can't believe this! Toby thought as he started to assemble his crossbow. *I'm about to take on a group of guttata. In the woods near Turtle Creek!* Then, before Toby could stifle the thought . . . *Maybe I should have stayed back at Killer Pizza.*

The Red Badge of Courage suddenly flashed in Toby's head. He had read Stephen Crane's classic just last year in English class. Would he be like the soldier in that story, turning and running like an idiot as soon as the battle began?

Enough! Toby scolded himself. *Don't even go there!*

Just as Toby finished assembling his crossbow a brisk wind blew through the trees. Thunder rumbled in the distance. The air had suddenly turned heavy, humid. A storm was on the way.

Toby snapped his arrow cartridge onto the crossbow, locked another into the receiving clip on his left bicep plate, then zeroed in on the guttata nearest him. Tracking the black-clad man in the dark was not easy. Toby lost him for a moment, then there he was again in CLOSE-UP, his intense features startling Toby. The man seemed to be *right there* in front of him, so close that Toby could make out a stream of saliva dripping down one side of his chin.

Disgusting!

The sight of the drooling guttata really unhinged Toby. The man began to jerk in and out of the crossbow scope, the result of Toby's suddenly shaking hands. Desperately trying to relocate his guttata, Toby instead found the form of the small boy, lying motionless on the ground near the fire. The sight of the boy went straight to Toby's heart.

Get it together, for God's sake! That's why you're here. For that kid!

Suddenly, everything seemed to happen at once. Harvey's high-pitched whistle cut through the night. Toby found his guttata and pulled the trigger.

Then the storm hit.

It was as though Toby's crossbow trigger had summoned the rain—*sheets* of it—to appear. It was like a magician's trick, the way the rain was all at once pounding down from the dark sky, snapping on the leaves of the tall oak trees and splashing on the ground with ferocious force.

Even through the falling rain, Toby was able to see that his arrow had flown wide of the mark. Two of the guttata flinched from the impact of Strobe's and Annabel's arrows, but they did not go down. The only guttata to fall was the one closest to Harvey. The rest of them scanned the woods, shock and anger showing in their dark eyes. Then Harvey appeared from his hiding place and was charging the black-clad group. Strobe and Annabel were a split second behind him.

Whoa! Is that what I'm supposed to do? Toby wondered. He hesitated, then jumped up and slung his crossbow over his shoulder.

Guess so!

And just like that, Toby found himself sprinting toward the battle that had broken out in front of him. The ground beneath was already slippery from the intense downpour. Churning through the wet underbrush, Toby saw Strobe tackle one of the black-clad figures and take him down. Annabel was already clashing with another one.

"TOBY!" Toby caught sight of Harvey through the falling rain. *"AFTER HIM!"* Harvey jerked his head in the direction of a figure that was heading up one side of the steep ravine, away from the action.

"GO!" Harvey commanded.

Blindly obeying Harvey's order, Toby changed direction and ran after the man. As he grabbed hold of a series of bushes to pull himself up the steep slippery hill, it felt to Toby as if the world around him was coming apart at the seams.

Lightning. Thunder. Drenching rain. From the bottom of the ravine came wild, alien-sounding screams, the guttata's battle cry. The shrieks made the hair at the back of Toby's neck stand on end.

This is totally insane!!! Toby thought as he made his way up the steep hill. When he arrived at the top—sopping wet and out of breath—Toby scanned the misty woods for the man who had retreated from the battle down below. At first he couldn't see him. Then, there he was, appearing from behind a wall of bare rock and heading for a large SUV parked among the trees. Toby went to one knee, took aim with his crossbow, and fired.

Toby was surprised to see the man fall. He hadn't hit the heart bull's-eye—necessary to kill a guttata—but rather, the man's leg, taking it right out from under him. Toby stood and ran toward the fallen man. He was almost there when the man slowly turned his head to look at him.

Toby skidded to a stop just as a crack of thunder exploded over his head, followed by a massive lightning flash that illuminated the forest like an X-ray. The instant of blinding light allowed Toby to see something horrifying.

The wounded man's eyes were completely red! No irises, no white. Just . . . red.

Toby staggered back from the sight. It was such a supernatural effect, those eyes, that Toby thought *his* eyes had played a trick on him. But they hadn't.

"Who are you?" the man asked. His voice sounded strange, as though it was being filtered through a device to camouflage his real voice.

Toby backed away—a feeling of dread rising—as the man slowly pulled himself to his feet. Except for those whacked-out eyes of his, he could have passed for a normal young person. A very handsome young person. Strong jaw. High cheekbones. The guy could be a *model*, if he weren't a guttata. Maybe he was a model. Toby suddenly thought he had seen this guy before. Yeah, he was sure he'd seen him!

Toby knew it was beyond weird to be wondering if he had seen this guy on a billboard or in the advertisement section of the local newspaper, even as his legs were turning to jelly from intense fear.

The man suddenly smiled. The rain was running down his face, distorting the smile, turning it even more sinister than it already was. "Had me running there for a moment, dude, I'll give you that. But I feel better now."

The man jerked his head back and forth, producing a loud crack. Then he took hold of the arrow imbedded in his leg and snapped it off, right at the point where the arrow entered the skin!

Toby thought he might faint, seeing that. What kind of strength would it take to break an arrow made of pure steel as though it were plastic? Without *flinching*?

"Can't escape, you know," the man coldly informed Toby, who continued to back away into the woods. "Your friends are already dead. Even if you were able to get away? We'd find you. That's 'cause we're *everywhere*, man. Let me save you the trouble of even trying to hide."

The man took a step toward Toby and held out a hand. "C'mere. I bet you're gonna taste just as good as that little kid."

Toby stared at the man's hand, mouth open in shock. At the end of each of the man's fingers and thumb . . . were three-inch-long talons!

That was enough for Toby. He whirled and ran back in the direction he had come. As he sprinted through the wet underbrush he turned and blindly fired his cross-bow. The arrow didn't hit its mark, but it did cause the man to dive out of its way, allowing Toby to put some well-needed distance between him and his pursuer.

He can't be right, Toby thought desperately as he approached the top of the hill that led back down into the ravine. *My friends can't be dead! They just can't be!*

When Toby reached the top of the hill, he leaped down the steep bank, his hands whirling for balance as his legs pounded through the underbrush. The slashing rain hit his face, making it hard to see more than a few feet in front of him. He couldn't see what was happening down below, but he thought he heard shouts and screams and those bloodcurdling battle cries. Bad as all that sounded, Toby was relieved when he heard the continuing sounds of battle. It was better than *silence*, that's for sure.

Toby suddenly felt sharp talons slash at his T-shirt. He cried out in surprise, changed direction, and charged to his right. Glancing wildly over his shoulder, Toby saw his pursuer slip on the slick hill as he tried to follow him, then disappear into the thick underbrush.

Through the mist and rain Toby was able to make out a huge fallen tree trunk up ahead. Skidding dangerously on the slick forest floor, Toby managed to reach the trunk.

He dove over it and hit the muddy ground on the other side with a thud. He crawled to the base of the tree, where the huge roots—looking like gnarled, ancient fingers, grasping for some unseen object—had pulled right up out of the ground. Here, there was a little space between the tree trunk and the ground, providing Toby with a protected view back in the direction where he had just been.

Toby switched the view on his crossbow from CLOSE-UP to WIDE, then looked into the scope to try to spot the man who had almost snatched him a few moments earlier. No sign of him. Toby moved the scope back and forth, desperately trying to get a bead on the guy.

Just then, the underbrush shook to Toby's right. Toby took aim at the telltale movement of the bushes and fired his arrow. Without waiting to see whether or not the arrow had found its mark, Toby fired another arrow. Then another.

He was about to fire once again when the man blasted up out of underbrush, right in front of him! Toby fell back in surprise. He couldn't believe it. There was *nothing human* left in the man! He had turned one hundred percent guttata!

The sight of the thing took Toby's breath away. Teeth the size of paring knives. Tightly coiled muscles under the irregularly spotted, leathery skin. An abnormally huge chest accenting its massive frame. With the rain and mud, thunder and flashes of lightning—plus the way the creature had appeared so suddenly from the bushes—Toby had the strange sensation that hell had split open and spit the thing right out into the woods.

And then, the thing-from-hell was coming right at him! Toby fired the final arrow in his cartridge, dove, and slid under the massive tree trunk. He yanked his knife from the sheath on his forearm plate and turned to meet the creature.

But instead of a taloned hand grabbing for him, Toby's eyes bulged when the guttata lifted the massive tree trunk right up off the ground! The few roots that were still attached to the earth snapped loose. Dirt flew into Toby's face.

The earth then exploded around Toby. The tree trunk crashed back to the muddy soil—missing Toby by mere inches—literally shaking the ground on impact. Toby cried out in pain as a sharp tree branch stabbed into his calf. He rolled away from the tree trunk, pulled himself to his feet, and launched himself down the hill.

Spotting a nearby tree that grew out of the steep hill at an odd 45-degree angle, Toby broke for it. He was certain he had no chance to outrun the guttata. The tree might provide him with a little protection. When he reached it he scrambled up the trunk like a hyper monkey.

Halfway up the trunk, Toby lodged himself between two thick branches and looked back toward the base of the tree. Expecting to see the guttata either coming for him or about to try to wrestle the tree right up out of the ground, Toby was shocked to see that the guttata was *retreating*. He couldn't believe it. There it was, heading back up the hill!

As Toby watched the creature disappear into the rain-soaked, misty forest, he suddenly felt woozy. He turned his leg to check out his injured calf. It was immediately obvious that the tear in his jeans wasn't the result of a tree branch. There were two tears—very sharp, not ragged—the resulting wound deep enough for the blood to flow freely.

The sounds at the bottom of the ravine had gotten softer, Toby realized. It was as though he had put in a couple of earplugs. But wait, the battle sounds below hadn't gotten softer, they had ceased altogether. *That's* why the guttata had retreated. His friends were okay! It was the *guttata* who had lost the battle!

At least Toby prayed that was the case. His vision was suddenly blurred, making it difficult to see as far as the bottom of the ravine. Toby reached up a hand— it looked to him as though he was moving in slow motion—to show his partners where he was. A weak raising of the hand was all Toby could muster. He tried to call out for help, but no sound emerged. It was as though his vocal cords were frozen.

Toby knew what was happening. He'd read all about the effects of a guttata bite in his textbook. As the rain continued to pound the woods, Toby thought how strange it was to be *sweating* in such an intense down-pour. He already had a fever. He was going fast and he knew it.

They'll never find me up in this tree, Toby thought as everything started to go dark around him. *How perfect is that? Up a tree!*

That was Toby's last thought before passing out.

9

"Toby?"

"Hey, c'mon, Tobe. Show us you're alive or something."

Toby opened his eyes slowly. He wasn't sure where he was at first. He was lying on a cot, that's the first thing that registered. Two hazy faces, staring down at him, was the second.

"There you go. I'll leave him with you, Annabel. Be right back."

When the one face moved away, Toby could see a nearby blackboard, the smell of the chalk reminding him of the time he had to stay after class in grade school and write "I will not forget my homework" fifty times.

Toby frowned. *Was* he back in grade school? That couldn't be right.

"Toby, how do you feel?"

The voice sounded familiar. Toby tried to place it. Just then, the pictures above the blackboard came into focus. A series of strange-looking monsters. The strong images cut through Toby's hazy state like a laser.

I'm in the Killer Pizza classroom, Toby realized.

And the person standing over him?

"Annabel?"

"Yeah, Toby, it's me. How do you feel?"

Like a jolt of electric shock therapy, the ordeal in the woods—every detail—suddenly flooded Toby's brain.

"What a horrible experience," Toby managed to say. "How is everyone?"

"Good."

"Anyone hurt?"

"Some scratches and cuts, but no one else was bitten."

"What about the guttata that was after me?"

"Don't worry about him."

"I *am* worried about him. Did he get away?"

Annabel hesitated before saying, "Yes. By the time we were able to go after him . . . he was gone."

Not good news. Toby suddenly remembered something else. "The boy?"

"Safe and sound. He was out the entire time. Which

is good for us. He didn't see a thing. Harvey told his parents he found him wandering around not far from his house."

Toby's double vision had eased and he was able to see Annabel more clearly. Her face was filthy. An area near her right ear was dotted with dried blood. Her T-shirt was mud stained and ripped, exposing the scratched chest plate beneath. Toby thought she looked great.

"I turned and ran," Toby said suddenly. "I couldn't handle it. Everything . . . it was just too much for me."

"You did fine."

"No, I didn't."

"You want to know something? I almost took off myself. I really did. Especially when my guy started turning guttata."

"I *did* take off. No 'almost' about it. I let my guy get away."

"You were all alone at the top of that hill, Toby. I had Strobe and Harvey on either side of me. That made a big difference, believe me."

Toby hadn't thought of that. Still, he knew he would have to deal with the disappointment of how he performed in his first Killer Pizza battle, at some point. For now, however . . .

"I need some water." Toby rose from his cot, then immediately lay back down.

"Dizzy?"

Toby nodded.

"Harvey said you might feel like that. It's as much from the shot he gave you as the bite."

"Harvey gave me a shot? Oh, right. The guttata antidote. Hey, wait a second. . . ." Toby glanced to his left. "Where's Chelsea?"

Her hospital bed was empty.

"She's okay," Annabel replied. "Well, not okay. But Harvey thinks he and Steve might have managed to save her."

"So where is she?"

"The hospital. Harvey's flying in the company doctor from Killer Pizza headquarters in New York. He'll be able to make sure she gets the proper care."

Toby felt a flood of relief at this news. Just then, Strobe came back into the classroom. He, too, was a mud-and-bloodstained mess. "Tobe! How's it goin'?" Toby couldn't believe how *exhilarated* Strobe looked. It was as though he'd just come back from seeing an extremely exciting movie instead of battling hybrids-from-hell.

"Glad to see you didn't die on us," Strobe said, smiling as he looked down at Toby. It was a rare thing, seeing

Strobe smile. A good fight with otherworldly creatures seemed to bring out the *light* side in Strobe's nickname.

"Hey, you notice something just now?" Strobe asked Toby.

Toby shook his head no. He was suddenly having a hard time keeping his eyes open.

"I called you Tobe."

Toby wasn't sure what Strobe was getting at.

"That's a nickname, right? Rhymes with Strobe."

Toby managed a weak smile. "Yeah, I guess you could call that a nickname."

"Was that something tonight, or what?" Strobe looked like he was ready to go out for another round with the guttata.

"It was something," Annabel agreed. But she didn't look charged up like Strobe did.

"Now what?" Toby suddenly asked.

The question had just kind of popped out. Toby had a feeling he was asking himself the question as much as he was asking Strobe and Annabel. It seemed to temporarily stump his KP partners.

Strobe was the one who offered an answer. "Now we need to get to that Alpha, pronto. Before the thing gets to us."

Good point. The Killer Pizza crew were in the midst

of a perilous cat-and-mouse game with the guttata, with each trying to locate the whereabouts of the other. Seeing as Toby's guttata had managed to escape, the guttata would now have a better idea of where their enemies lived. Not the most comforting thought.

"Let us worry about that right now, Toby," Annabel said. "You just need to concentrate on getting better."

Yeah, first things first, Toby thought. He wanted to talk to Annabel and Strobe a bit longer, but before he knew it his eyes had closed. He struggled to stay awake, but simply couldn't. Drifting off to sleep, it wasn't long before Toby had entered a strange dream landscape.

Unfortunately, many nasty things lurked there, ready to pounce on him.

PART THREE:
STAKEOUTS, NEW RECIPES, AND VISITORS IN THE NIGHT

1

"NO!!!"

Toby woke up instantly, sweating and out of breath. Staring into the darkness that shrouded his bedroom, he instinctively rubbed his shoulder where the Alpha guttata had grabbed him. The pain in Toby's nightmare had felt so real that it had shattered his dream, snapping him back to the here and now.

The monstrous guttata's talons piercing his skin was the flash point where Toby *always* woke up, this not being the first time he had been subjected to this particular nightmare.

"Oh, man!" Toby said in dismay. "When is this gonna stop?"

This had been going on for the past week. Toby was still on leave from Killer Pizza, recovering from his guttata bite. The first few nights had been especially difficult—and strange—with Toby thrashing about in bed, groaning, sweating, and occasionally calling out in his sleep, "I'm changing! I'm changing!"

Fortunately, Toby hadn't been changing. Harvey's antidote had worked. Since those first few nights, however, Toby's nightmares had dissolved from a crazy quilt of terrifying images into the same dependable scenario: Toby being chased through a strange, apocalyptic landscape by a terrifying Alpha guttata, the thing flying a few feet from the ground as it closed in on him.

Of course Toby hadn't been able to explain to his parents what really happened the night he spent on a cot in Killer Pizza's classroom, which meant his mother was convinced that his lingering symptoms were the result of . . . well, she didn't even want to *think* about what her son had been up to. The bottom line was that Toby had been grounded for a week. He had three more days of house arrest, then he would be free to go back to Killer Pizza.

Toby lay back on his pillow and stared up at the ceiling. He knew he would have a difficult time getting back to sleep. The intense nightmares were hard to shake. They were unlike anything Toby had ever experienced before. The sights, sounds, smells . . . everything in the dreams felt so *real*. But the nightmares also felt like a warning. A preview of something that was actually going to happen.

Very creepy. And very unsettling.

Still rubbing the imaginary wound on his shoulder, Toby closed his eyes. Immediately, he could see the final image in his nightmare. The Alpha's taloned hand, ripping into him. The talons looked to be at least a *foot long*, making the one Toby had found in his backyard look . . . well, like a pup's. Toby wondered if the real Alpha's talons were as big as they were in his dream. If so, there was one thing he was certain of: He didn't want any part of the thing. No way.

■ ■ ■

On the last night before returning to Killer Pizza, Toby took advantage of a rare evening of peace and quiet—his sister was at a sleepover and his parents were at the movies—to try out the Pizza Rustica recipe he had written down in his notebook the previous week.

Yes, Toby was putting on his apron and taking out the pots and pans. There was a very particular reason for his kitchen session, beyond just wanting to experiment with a new recipe. Toby had been surprised and pleased to discover that cooking actually *calmed* him.

Even in the crazy KP kitchen, after the first week, anyway, it was as though he was able to develop a kind of tunnel vision, focusing on the task at hand without freaking out, like he usually did when confronted with stressful situations.

So Toby was able to temporarily leave behind all thoughts of guttata and Alphas and deadly talons as he worked. When the Pizza Rustica was done, he pulled it gently out of the oven. Crust? Perfect. Aroma? Pretty tasty-smelling. Overall presentation? Toby nodded in approval. The pizza looked terrific. But now came the real test. Toby waited for the pizza to cool, then cut a slice of the multilayered pizza pie, closed his eyes, and took a bite.

Mmmmmm. Good. Very good, actually. Spinach, garlic, bell peppers, prosciutto, pepperoni, salami. Terrific! Toby was pleased that the Pizza Rustica tasted as good as it had looked on the program.

Double *mmmmmmm!!!*

Toby's pizza high didn't last long, however. As he cleaned up the kitchen, his good mood started to fade. The question that had been eating at him all week long was raising its hand once again, demanding attention.

What to do the following morning, upon his return

to Killer Pizza? Toby had gone back and forth during his time off. One option was simply not resuming his training, letting Strobe and Annabel carry on without him. Toby felt like he was dragging his partners down.

But then, as Annabel said that day in Prospect Park, *somebody* had to take on these monsters. Toby just wasn't sure that he was cut out be one of those somebodies.

So . . . stay or leave? Toby had one more night to make his decision.

■ ■ ■

Walking up to Harvey's office, Toby paused for a moment, then opened the door and went inside. Harvey was sitting behind his desk, immersed in paperwork. He gave Toby a brisk nod as he entered.

"Welcome back."

"Thanks. Yeah, it's good to be back."

"You wanted to see me about something?"

Hands clasped behind his back, Toby shifted nervously. He'd gone over what he was about to say more than a few times.

"I don't have all day, Toby."

"Sure. Of course." Toby cleared his throat, then said, "I'm withdrawing from the Killer Pizza Academy."

Harvey didn't say anything. The silence quickly became uncomfortable. Toby couldn't tell if Harvey was looking at him or *past* him, at something on the other side of the office.

"I don't accept your resignation," Harvey finally said.

Not what Toby was expecting to hear. Harvey indicated the seat near his desk. "Sit. Please."

Toby sat.

"For one thing, at this point I can't let you go. You already know too much about the program. I'd have to kill you."

Toby managed a short laugh, but his smile faded when Harvey's deadpan expression didn't change. The guy was serious!

"Just kidding," Harvey said, revealing a rare sense of humor. "Tell me why you want to resign."

Expecting just such a question, Toby had rehearsed his answer, but it didn't come out the way he'd planned. "That night in the woods . . . I don't know, I just . . . It's not something I ever want to go through again. I've been having nightmares ever since. Really bad ones. Besides, I didn't do that great of a job, anyway. I mean, I let the guy get away. Now the guttata know where we live. The general area, anyway."

"Not necessarily. I covered our tracks pretty well before we left the woods. I don't believe they'll be able to sniff us out."

"The bottom line, sir, after giving it a lot of thought . . . I just don't think I have what it takes to be an MCO."

"I believe you're wrong about that, Toby."

"I don't get it. I mean, what is it you see in me? It's not like I'm 'The One' or anything. I haven't noticed any telltale marks on my body, you know? I'm just an average kind of kid."

"Who is making the mistake of comparing himself to Annabel and Strobe."

"Yeah, I guess I am."

"You can't do that. Those two are extraordinarily talented."

"So what am I? You said the other day you thought I had qualities I didn't know about. I mean, name one." Toby laughed a short laugh, as though that would be difficult for Harvey to do.

Harvey stood and came around his desk. "I've learned to trust my instincts over the years, Toby. In your case, I believe you have depths of strength, physical and mental, you haven't even begun to tap into."

147

"So, what . . . ? This is just a feeling of yours?"

"No, not just a feeling. You have to remember I spent three weeks with you in the KP kitchen. I had plenty of time to observe you at work, up close and personal. You'd be surprised how much you can learn about a person, if you really *study* them."

"And what you learned was . . . I'm a closet Hulk."

"Let's not get carried away. Superhero? No. Depths of inner strength? Yes. Definitely. My job now is to help you tap into that strength. It's there, believe me. It's a cliché, I know, but once *you* start believing it's there . . . that's when things happen. That's when you really start to grow."

Toby was silent.

"Don't worry about the way you reacted in the woods. It's perfectly understandable. You couldn't have asked for a more intense experience your first time out. The more you do this, the more seasoned you become. It gets easier, believe me."

"But what about the nightmares?" Toby asked. "They seem so real. Will they ever go away?"

Harvey hesitated before answering. Toby thought he saw the answer to his question in Harvey's eyes, but it wasn't the one Harvey said out loud. "Yes, they do."

In an instant, Toby saw his boss in a different way. A more *human* way. The look in Harvey's eyes suggested someone who had been wounded—literally and figuratively—more than a few times in the course of carrying out his chosen "profession." Then the look was gone and Harvey's usual brusque manner returned.

"This is what I suggest," Harvey said. "Stick it out through the training period before making your decision."

Toby wasn't sure what to say. It certainly was nice to get some encouragement for a change. His teachers at school hardly ever did that. But Toby couldn't help thinking there must be an easier way to get a pat on the back than battling monstrous guttata!

"I'll cut your training back to four times a week," Harvey added. "The other two days, you can work up in the kitchen."

Toby looked at Harvey in surprise. Work up in the kitchen? What a tantalizing offer!

"That's the best I can do. Take it or leave it."

Toby couldn't resist. "Okay," he said, then he stood, awkwardly holding out his hand to seal the deal. Harvey shook Toby's hand and returned to his seat. When he looked up at Toby, he seemed surprised that he was still in his office.

"Don't you have self-defense class?"

"Uh . . . yeah."

Harvey nodded, his expression suggesting that Toby get to it. Toby hesitated a moment, then exited the office, closing the door softly behind him on his way out.

2

The black Hummer contained four people. The blue-
eyed woman sat in the backseat with the young guttata Toby had confronted in the woods. The driver was
Thomas Gome. As for the person in the front passenger
seat, he looked to be somewhere in his forties. Maybe
younger. No, wait, older. Hold on . . . younger. Definitely younger.

Actually, it was difficult to pinpoint the man's age. It
depended on how the light from the passing streetlamps
hit his face. That, and the contrast between the man's
ruggedly handsome, youthful features and his hair—his
most distinguishing characteristic—of *pure silver*.

If the man's age was difficult to lock down, one thing
was immediately obvious about him. He oozed charisma.
The dangerous variety. Sitting very still—unnervingly
so—he radiated a coiled, ominous kind of energy.

"I'm telling you, we've gone all over these woods. . . ."

The silver-haired man did not have to say a word to silence the younger man in the backseat. A glance in his direction was more than enough to do the trick.

There were no more words spoken as Gome negotiated the twisting turns in the heavily wooded area east of the city. The digital clock on the dashboard indicated that it was three o'clock in the morning.

■ ■ ■

Gome and the blue-eyed woman took their time as they walked through the fern-carpeted floor of the woods. They studied—*sniffed*—the area around them, taking in every detail. After they had completed their search, they returned to where they had started. The young guttata and the silver-haired man were waiting for them. Along with almost two dozen other men and women, who had also been searching the woods. Spread out under the cathedral-like canopy of the tall oaks, they looked like a creepy platoon of black-clad soldiers, ready to do battle.

"Nothing, right?" the young guttata asked.

The blue-eyed woman shook her head. Not a thing.

"What kind of humans can wipe out their scent?" the young guttata wanted to know. "I mean, who are we dealing with here?"

The silver-haired man slowly focused his gaze on the young guttata. "The only reason we're here tonight is because you and your recently deceased comrades disobeyed one of my orders."

The young guttata looked like he had instantly stopped breathing, his eyes reflecting how petrified he was at suddenly being singled out by the silver-haired man.

"Do you remember what it was that I said?" the silver-haired man asked. "Or shall I remind you?"

"No, sir. I remember."

"What was that? I couldn't hear you."

"I remember what you said, sir."

"Which was?"

"We were not to congregate after dark until further notice."

"And why was that?"

"Because of the attack on our comrade."

"Correct. No congregating after dark until further notice. I don't recall giving notice on that particular order, do you?"

"No, sir."

The blue-eyed woman had taken a position just to the left of the young guttata. Something at the end of her hand glinted in the moonlight as her arm suddenly lashed out in a wide arc in the direction of the young man. He didn't know what hit him. His instantly lifeless body stood upright for a moment, then crumpled to the ground.

The shocking attack elicited an audible response from the rest of the guttata. They hadn't seen this coming. All eyes were now focused on the single talon that extended from the woman's index finger. That's what had caused the glint in the moonlight, what had found just the right spot on the young guttata's neck to take his life. The woman showed no emotion as the talon slowly morphed back into a normal fingernail.

"I will not tolerate anyone disobeying one of my orders," the silver-haired man informed his elite group of soldiers. "My only consideration is for our safety, our continued well-being. Which brings me to the people who eliminated one of our most valued colleagues. I can assure you they are mere amateurs compared to others I have faced. Our colleague's death will be avenged. I guarantee it."

The silver-haired man looked at the dark figures spread out among the trees for a moment, then he turned and walked away from them. Gome and the blue-eyed woman followed him.

The group in the woods slowly dispersed. Two of the guttata approached the lifeless body and dragged it off by the legs, as though it were a dead animal instead of a former comrade. The executed man was clearly persona non grata. Already forgotten.

All that remained was to dispose of the body.

3

"Let's review our current situation."

Harvey sliced a tomato and tossed it into the Ghoul-
ishous Salad. Before, it had been the deliveryman's de-
sertion that caused Harvey to change the classroom
setting. This time Harvey had abruptly fired the entire afternoon kitchen staff. The temporary solution had been
to press his rookies back into cooking duty, at least until
the evening shift arrived.

"One . . ." Harvey continued. "Chelsea Travers was
one of our guttata's victims. The other is still at large.
Two . . . so far, Steve and I have had no success locating
the Alpha. This puts us in a defensive position, which is
not where I want to be."

As Annabel passed by Harvey with a couple of piz-
zas for the new deliveryman—waiting at the counter—
Harvey put his salad in a bag and gave it to her. Then
Annabel returned to the kitchen.

"Fortunately, the pack's Gathering is on the horizon," Harvey said. "Anyone know when it is?"

"Five days?" Strobe guessed.

"Six. It just might be the thing we need to get to the Alpha. Anyone know why?"

Nobody answered right away, but then Annabel said, "First, we have to find Sammy's other victim."

Strobe and Toby frowned. They didn't see how that would help them. But Harvey nodded appreciatively at Annabel's answer.

"Very good, Annabel. If we can discover who the other person was that our guttata infected, we will be able to keep a watch on its house. The new guttata, after its transformation, after being trained by its donor, will return to its home, in human form, of course . . ."

". . . and come the new moon, we follow this person to the monthly Gathering, where we will definitely find Alpha Man," Strobe said, finishing off Harvey's sentence for him. "Excellent, Annabel."

Annabel gave Strobe a thank-you smile.

Harvey produced a small stack of newspapers and distributed one paper to each of his students. "This is today's edition. Page forty-nine. The article in the lower right-hand corner. I'll take over here while you read it."

The trio opened their newspapers as Harvey slid a

couple of pizzas into the oven, then exited the kitchen to answer the phone. The title of the article was "Hidden Hills Man Goes Missing." The missing man was a 20-year-old named Chris Child. He had mysteriously disappeared earlier in the week.

"It's possible that Child is the other victim," Harvey said after he had taken the phone order and placed it on the wheel. "What we have to do before staking out his house, however, is confirm that Child is definitely our man. Otherwise we'll just be wasting our time. His home is located at 419 Finney Drive. As soon as the night shift gets here, that is your destination."

"I thought you said we had to confirm Child was our guy before staking out his house," Strobe said.

"You will not be watching his house tonight, Strobe. What you will be doing is conducting Killer Pizza's version of a search warrant."

Just then a punker with red-tipped hair entered the shop. "Anyone here? I need a dozen Mummy Wraps!"

4

Earlier in the week, a police car had been a familiar
sight in front of 419 Finney Drive. But after getting the information they needed, the police were no longer around.
They had left with a solemn promise to call Mrs. Child if
they discovered anything about her missing son.

Carrying one Killer Pizza Frankensausage, medium-
size, Strobe was struck by the lonesome vibe of the house
as he walked up the quaint, flower-lined path to the front
door. Harvey had dropped him off and was now parked
down the street, monitoring the unfolding KP "search
warrant."

Behind the house, Toby and Annabel were already in
position and in contact with Strobe via wireless headsets. "I'm approaching the front door," the two heard
Strobe relay from the front of the house. A few moments
later: "I'm ringing the bell." Toby and Annabel tensed as
they got ready for Strobe's command.

"Go!"

Instantly breaking from their hiding place, the two ran toward the back door.

Meanwhile, the middle-aged woman who had just opened the front door was clearly confused that a Killer Pizza deliveryman had just rung her doorbell. "Yes?" she asked.

Strobe's heart immediately went out to Chris Child's mother. She did not look good. Her face was drawn. Her eyes showed deep fatigue. But Strobe had a job to do, and he wasn't about to let his sympathy for Mrs. Child get in the way of that.

"You ordered a pizza?" he asked.

"No. I did not order a pizza."

It was Strobe's turn to look confused. "Are you sure? I have the order form right here. . . ." Strobe started to look through his pockets, taking his good old time in the process.

As Strobe employed his stalling tactic, Annabel was using the techniques she had learned from a crash course in burglary just before heading out to Mrs. Child's house to unlock the back door. Accomplishing that, she stepped into the kitchen. Toby was right behind her. They walked quietly on soft-soled sneakers through the kitchen, the dining room, and into the living room. They could now hear Strobe at the open front door.

"I'm certain it was 419 Finney Drive. Yes! Here's the order form."

"Well, there's been a mistake. I did not order a pizza."

"Jeez, this is really unusual. We simply do not make mistakes at Killer Pizza."

"You did this time. I'm sorry, but if you'll excuse me . . ."

Annabel and Toby had arrived at the end of a hallway that led to the front entrance and a set of stairs that led to the second floor. The stairs were halfway between where Annabel and Toby stood and the front door. Mrs. Child's back was to them, but she was about to close the door and terminate the discussion about the mistaken pizza order.

Strobe saw Annabel and Toby at the end of the hall. He quickly jammed his shoulder against the door to prevent Mrs. Child from closing it. "My cell is dead. Do you mind if I call my supervisor? I'm sure he'll be able to clear this up."

Taking advantage of Strobe's last-gasp effort to prevent Mrs. Child from closing the door in his face,

Annabel and Toby scampered down the hall and up to the second floor.

Mrs. Child couldn't resist Strobe's open, innocent-looking smile. "There's a phone in the living room," she said, stepping away from the door. "You may use that."

"Thank you very much."

Crouching behind the upstairs banister, Annabel waited until Strobe and Mrs. Child had disappeared into the living room, then silently indicated to Toby that she would take the rooms to the right of the stairs. Toby's search would consist of the rooms to the left.

They were there to gather anything that belonged to Chris Child—toothbrush, hairs on a pillowcase, a razor—that could be tested forensically to confirm that Child was, indeed, the victim of a guttata bite.

Toby entered the bedroom nearest the stairs and snapped down his NVGs to be able to see in the dark room. The room was a mess. The bed unmade. The air had a musty, stale smell. Toby pulled on a pair of thin sanitary gloves as he crossed the room to the bathroom. He took several plastic bags from a pouch on his belt.

There was a toothbrush in a glass on the sink. Toby put the toothbrush in one of the plastic bags. He spotted a shaver lying on a nearby shelf. He picked it up, placed a plastic bag over its head, and gave the shaver a jarring upside-down shake. After replacing the shaver and shoving the evidence bags into his pouch, Toby turned to leave the bathroom.

"WHOA!" he shouted, practically leaping out of his sneakers. Annabel was right behind him!

"Shhhhhhhh!" Annabel slapped her hand over Toby's mouth. The two stood like statues, waiting to hear if there was any reaction downstairs to Toby's shout of alarm.

There was. Very faintly they heard Mrs. Child say, "I'm certain I heard something upstairs."

"Crap. What do we do?" Toby whispered.

"Just wait," Annabel commanded.

The two listened as Strobe said, "I didn't hear anything."

"There's somebody up there," Mrs. Child insisted.

"Maybe *I* should go up," Strobe suggested. "Better yet, maybe you should call the police."

"It's probably my son," Mrs. Child replied, her voice hopeful, and louder this time. She sounded like she was right at the bottom of the stairs! Annabel and Toby, their faces close together, held their breath.

"I don't think it's a good idea for you to go up there alone," Strobe said.

"I appreciate your concern, young man, but it's perfectly all right. I'm sure it's Chris. He always comes in the back way. You can let yourself out, if you don't mind."

Annabel and Toby heard Mrs. Child's footsteps coming up the stairs. *Clomp. Clomp. Clomp.*

"We're outta here!!!" Toby hissed frantically.

"The bedroom window!" Annabel hissed back, then quickly led the way into the bedroom and opened the window. The white curtains, billowing inward from the night breeze, looked like dual dancing ghosts.

Annabel stepped through the window and onto the roof. Toby quickly followed. He pulled the window down and ducked out of sight just as Mrs. Child came into the bedroom.

"Chris?" Mrs. Child called out. Toby thought it was the saddest sound he'd ever heard, that one word. And he felt bad for making Mrs. Child think that her son had returned home.

Turning away from the window, Toby saw an obvious escape route: a large tree in the backyard of the Child house. It would take a slight leap to make it to the tree's branches that reached out across the yard toward the roof. Nothing too dangerous.

"You go first," Annabel said.

Toby made the jump, then looked back at Annabel. Instead of leaping from the roof, Annabel looked like her feet were glued to it.

"Annabel? You okay?"

Clearly Annabel wasn't okay. She looked absolutely petrified. "Maybe now's not the time to mention this," she said. "But I'm afraid of heights."

Toby had to stifle a smile. Annabel—the quick study, the can-do person, the actual descendant of a sixteenth-century samurai, maybe—was afraid of heights? It didn't seem possible.

"I see you smiling," Annabel said, looking embarrassed as she clung to the eave of a dormer roof overhang.

"No, I'm not."

"Just . . . get me out of here, okay?"

5

After repeated encouragement from Toby, Annabel did manage the leap from roof to tree, after which she and Toby were able to make their getaway. Driving away from the Child house, Harvey congratulated the trio on the success of their first Killer Pizza "search warrant."

Two days later, after testing hair and skin samples from Child's shaver and comparing it to the DNA in the blood from Sammy's system, Harvey was able to confirm that Chris Child was, indeed, the victim of a guttata bite.

"Stakeout time," Strobe said after hearing the news.

"That's right," Harvey replied. "Two of you at a time. One three-hour shift a night, starting at sunset. Steve and I will take turns on the long midnight to six A.M. shift."

"What about the daylight hours?" Annabel asked.

She and Toby, Strobe, Harvey, and Steve were all gathered in Harvey's downstairs office.

"Doubtful Child will return to his house during the day. His eyes will be especially sensitive for some time after the transformation. Who wants to take tonight's shift?"

Annabel and Strobe immediately raised their hands. Harvey nodded. "Off with you. It's already dark. See you at midnight. Be sure to take all of your gear. The guttata are also interested in finding out who their lost comrade infected, assuming they already haven't. Be on the lookout for them, as well."

As the group started to break up, an intercom on the wall crackled to life. "Steve, we need some help!" a harried voice said. "A Little League team just arrived. It's a traffic jam!"

The workers overhead thought the intercom connected them to Steve's office on the first floor, where he was never to be disturbed.

"Mind taking it, Toby?" Steve asked.

Of course, Toby didn't mind taking it. He walked up the spiral staircase, pushed through the door into the storage room, and walked down the hall to the kitchen. Putting on his apron, Toby looked around with a frown.

"No wonder you're having a meltdown," he said to the frenzied cook next to him. "You're short a man."

"Yeah, Ryan called in sick."

Toby immediately stopped what he was doing. "Sick? What, does he have a cold or something?"

"Don't know. He sounded terrible, though. Couldn't even get out of bed. He's not sure what he has."

Toby's senses suddenly seemed hyperactive. He excused himself and headed back downstairs. Did the guy just have a cold? Or the flu, maybe? Somehow Toby didn't think so. He knew he needed to tell Harvey about his sick Killer Pizza employee, that's for sure.

Double-timing it down the spiral staircase, two words reverberated in Toby's brain. Two chilling words that had been spoken to him that horrible night in the woods:

We're everywhere.

■ ■ ■

The Child house was located at the bottom of Prospect Park, the park where Toby, Annabel, and Strobe had made their collective decision to sign up for the MCO Academy. A large stand of bushes bordered one side of the park, and that's where Annabel and Strobe set up their stakeout. They hollowed out a portion of the bushes, creating a small cave-like area that was completely hidden from passersby, then sat down to watch the house below.

When Steve appeared three hours later, Strobe and Annabel had nothing to report. There had been no sign of suspicious activity anywhere in the neighborhood. It was now Steve's turn to sit in the claustrophobic, leafy cavern. He settled in for the long midnight-to-dawn shift.

■ ■ ■

As Strobe and Annabel headed home from their inaugural Killer Pizza stakeout, Chris Child was resting in a hollow that he had carved out from a short bluff that bordered one of the streams near North Park.

Child's bizarre transformation, which had begun a few days ago, had already distorted his features to a hair-raising, alarming degree. Strangely enough, Child felt pretty good at this point in his otherworldly voyage. Physically, anyway. He was *confused* about what was happening to him, to be sure, but he felt stronger than he ever had in his entire life. Not only that, the scents and sounds in the woods beyond his self-made cave were sharper and more exciting than anything Child had ever experienced before. It was like a natural high.

So now, Child—a rather unnerving-looking combination of human-guttata—was waiting. The same instinct that had instructed him to seek a private place to complete his transformation also told him that someone—some*thing*—was coming to help him.

But a spark of human impulse still resided in Chris. A spark that continued to whisper . . . *go home*. Chris resisted the pull of that human call. He sensed it was too soon to go back to his "nest."

Another deeply imbedded human impulse caused Chris to look at his watch. Ooops. When would he stop doing that? The Swatch timepiece had slipped off a few days ago when Chris's arm had begun to grow longer. And bonier.

Chris grunted—more a guttata sound than human—in exasperation. He knew that he was more than a little whacked-out. He didn't know if he was coming or going. He *did* know that his life had changed in a most far-out and unexpected way.

After all, just last month he'd been working at the Echo 8-Plex Theaters down on Streets Run. From that . . . to *this*. A detour totally beyond weird.

Unfortunately, as much as the former Chris Child might want to go back to his former life, there was nothing he could do at this point but sit and wait. In the damp hollow of his cave. And fight that premature urge to *go back home*.

6

"No, Carl! Absolutely not!"

"We already punished him once, Jean. I say we let the boy stay home."

"Why, so he can have a bunch of *wild parties* while we're gone?"

Toby was listening from his bedroom as his parents argued about whether or not to allow him to stay home when they went on their annual vacation to Orlando, which would kick off the following morning.

Toby had no intention of going. He was getting too old to go on vacations with his family. Besides, he had important work to do at Killer Pizza. But at this point it sounded like his mom wasn't budging. After his "all-nighter," she clearly didn't trust him to stay home alone.

Toby didn't stick around to hear the resolution to his parents' battle. He had some free time before heading off to Prospect Park—where he and Annabel would be taking the sunset-to-midnight stakeout shift—and had decided to go see Chelsea in the hospital.

Unfortunately, after briefly showing signs of improvement, Chelsea had started to weaken. The stress and strain of the guttata bite had apparently been too much for her. The KP doctor wasn't even sure if Chelsea was going to make it, a supremely depressing thought for Toby.

He took a detour on his bike ride to the hospital to buy some flowers. He'd never visited anyone in the hospital before, but he thought that's what you were supposed to do. Bring flowers with you.

As Toby walked toward Chelsea's hospital room, a nurse passed him in the hall. Toby froze and glanced over his shoulder at the nurse. He thought he had just seen the nurse's left hand shaking! Toby studied the nurse as she walked down the hall, away from him. Her hand looked okay, now. Still, Toby was pretty sure. . . .

She's okay, Toby tried to convince himself. *Check it out. She looks perfectly fine.*

There was a very good reason for Toby's hypersensitivity to anything that looked suspiciously "guttata-like," besides the fact that he'd been thinking about practically nothing else *but* guttata for the past month. Harvey had called Toby just a few hours earlier to inform him that he had paid a visit to Killer Pizza's sick employee. All signs pointed to the young man being a guttata-bite victim.

So, yes, the screws were tightening. The pressure building. Now, more than ever, it really did feel to Toby as though the guttata were everywhere and were closing in on him and his KP partners.

The nurse had stopped to talk to a doctor. Toby waited a moment to see if the telltale shaking of the left hand reappeared. When it didn't, he turned and approached Chelsea's room. He would inquire about the nurse's name after seeing Chelsea. That's what he'd do. That way Harvey could check up on her, just to be sure.

After a final look down the hall at the nurse, Toby knocked on Chelsea's door. He cautiously entered the room when no one answered. Chelsea was lying in bed, asleep. Hooked up to a number of monitors, she didn't look much different from the last time Toby had seen her. Seeing Chelsea like this gave Toby a hopeless and empty feeling. He looked around the room, placed his flowers on a nearby shelf, then wasn't sure what to do. Leave? Wait to see if Chelsea woke up?

Toby decided to stay for a while. Sitting in a chair near the bed, watching Chelsea, hearing her strained, raspy breath, Toby's low spirits were suddenly pushed aside by a shot of anger. It wasn't fair, what had happened to Chelsea. She didn't ask for this.

"Who're you?"

Toby was jolted out of his thoughts by Chelsea's whispered question. Her eyes were barely open, as though it were a strain just to keep her lids at half-mast.

"I'm . . . Toby. Toby Magill."

Chelsea's eyes narrowed as she studied him. "Oh, yeah, right. You were at The Zone the other night."

Toby nodded. He had been informed that Chelsea's recent memory was spotty at best.

"What are you doin' here?"

"I heard you were in the hospital, so . . . I figured I'd come visit."

"Pretty flowers. You bring 'em?"

"Yeah."

"What kind are they?"

"I'm not sure."

"They smell good."

Chelsea's eyes started to close. "It's real sweet of you to come. Hardly anyone's been by to see me."

"Well . . . I'm happy I stopped by."

Chelsea didn't respond. Her eyes had closed and she looked like she had fallen back asleep. But then she frowned and looked at Toby.

"What's wrong?"

"I remember you asking me if anything had bitten me. How did you know that?"

"I don't know . . . a wild guess?"

"No, it wasn't, was it? You know. You know what bit me."

Toby was silent.

"You have to tell me. I was so out of it that night, I think I told the doctor I'd been bitten by an *alien*. Should have seen his face. All I want to know is . . . was I just seeing things? Am I crazy? I really don't know anymore."

Toby sensed a kind of desperation in Chelsea to know the answer to her question. He couldn't deny her.

"You're not crazy, Chelsea. But it wasn't an alien that bit you. It was a monster."

■ ■ ■

A half hour later, Toby was walking down the hospital hallway. Chelsea had fallen asleep right after he had revealed to her that monsters did exist, and that she'd met one of them. Chelsea had not looked surprised when Toby told her that. Matter-of-fact, it seemed to Toby as though she had gained a small amount of peace from the news. She wasn't crazy, after all.

Turning a corner, Toby suddenly stopped in his tracks. He couldn't believe what he was seeing. *Lenny* and a few of his pals were coming toward him!

Toby wasn't sure what to do. Continue down the hall or head in the opposite direction? Lenny gave him a blank look as he approached. The bully didn't recognize him! But then the bald-headed tough's eyes sparked darkly when he was almost shoulder to shoulder with Toby.

Toby walked quickly past Lenny, avoiding his glare. The last thing he wanted right now was another confrontation with this guy. He had more important things to do.

"Hey, dude. Where you think you're going?" Lenny said the words low and cold. Toby continued on down the hall. No way was he going to respond to Lenny's question. "The more important question," Lenny continued. "Where you comin' *from*?" Suddenly, just like the night at the Fun Zone, Toby felt Lenny grab him painfully from behind.

This time Toby's reaction was slightly different.

Using the most elementary of martial arts moves he

had learned in class, Toby spun around, at the same time jerking up his right arm to knock Lenny's hand away from his shoulder.

BAM!!!

Toby followed his spin with a clenched left fist, palm-down shot to Lenny's chest. Lenny staggered back from the short, powerful punch, his mouth forming an O of surprise.

Toby should have left it at that. But he wasn't thinking clearly. Heck, he wasn't thinking at all. He had snapped into a *zone.* He was executing a combination of moves that Steve had drilled into him.

So Toby twirled to his right, bringing his leg up and out as he executed his martial arts pirouette.

GOMPH!!!

Toby's right foot slammed into Lenny's jaw, dropping him instantly to the floor. As though coming out of a trance, Toby looked down in surprise at Lenny's inert body.

Whoa! He'd never been able to do *that* in class!

■ ■ ■

The hospital security guard was summoned. Then the police. As Toby sat silently in the small security guard's office waiting for the police to arrive, two very different emotions were duking it out inside him.

Toby couldn't help but feel a certain amount of pride at being able to deal with the older and more powerful Lenny Baker.

But he also felt badly about what he had done. One of the first things he learned from Steve in self-defense class was the importance of self-control in the martial arts. He had taken his confrontation with Lenny, who had suffered a dislocated jaw, too far, that's for sure.

When the police arrived they questioned Lenny's pals and Toby about what had happened. They quickly bought Toby's version of the story. Lenny's pals' spin on the events—that Toby had attacked Lenny, unprovoked—was pretty easy to discount, especially considering Lenny and his gang's spotty reputation. So, checking this one off as a clear-cut case of self-defense, Toby was not escorted to the police station and booked with assault. But the police did call Toby's father, who came to the hospital to take his son back home.

■ ■ ■

Toby and his father were silent as Mr. Magill drove along the twisting streets of Hidden Hills. Toby could only imagine what was going through his dad's head.

"I really need to get new windshield wipers," Mr. Magill said. A summer shower had greeted Toby and his dad when they came out of the hospital. Toby looked over to see his father squinting to see past the streaks on the windshield caused by the faulty wipers.

"Is that really what you're thinking about, Dad? Getting new windshield wipers? I mean, after what just happened?"

Mr. Magill was silent. Toby wasn't sure if his dad was going to respond to his question. "You know, Toby . . ." Mr. Magill finally said. "I'm not sure what to say. What would *you* say if a policeman gave you a call to let you know your son just leveled a kid with a kick to the head? Keep in mind that you didn't even know that your son was taking any kind of martial arts classes."

"I don't know," Toby had to admit.

"There you go."

More silence in the car. Then . . .

"I will say this. You've been quite a surprise to me this summer. You've certainly changed over the past couple months, that's for sure."

"Changed?"

"Absolutely. Physically, of course, I already noticed that. You never looked better, Toby. But it's more than just those muscles of yours. I think it's your job. It's made you more responsible. More confident." Mr. Magill suddenly frowned. "But then you go and pull off a stunt like your 'all-nighter.' And now, tonight. It's a little confusing, I have to admit. I'm not sure who I'm dealing with, day to day, Toby."

Toby wished he could tell his dad about that "all-nighter." Maybe one of these days, he would be able to.

"Anyway, you really took that guy down, huh?"

"Yes, I guess I did."

"Well . . . watch that foot of yours in the future. Okay?"

That was the end of the lecture, Toby realized. From his dad, anyway. His mom would be a different story. No matter what went down in that particular conversation, Toby had every intention of sneaking out afterward to join Annabel on the stakeout. No way was he going to let his KP partner sit all by herself for three hours, watching the Child house.

7

At the same time Annabel was sitting in her hiding
place, studying the Child house and waiting for Toby to
arrive, the blue-eyed woman was walking down a dark,
deserted coal mine tunnel located a few miles east of
North Park. Her superior sense of smell and hearing,
more so than sight, allowed her to navigate the pitch-
dark passageway.

Except for the night in the woods with her Alpha
leader a few days ago, the woman had spent all of her
time trying to locate her fallen comrade's two marks. After checking out a fistful of the missing persons reports,
she had finally locked on to a trail that first led her to a
hollowed-out cave in North Park, then to this abandoned
coal mine.

Turning a corner, the woman sensed a large cav-
ernous area up ahead. Approaching the cave-like

expansion at the end of the tunnel, she entered cautiously. She didn't want to spook the mark.

Several mounds of discarded, left-behind coal dotted the cavern. Sniffing audibly like an aroused animal, the woman zeroed in on one of the mounds. She walked toward it, circled around to the other side, and discovered . . .

Nothing. The woman's luminous blue eyes narrowed as she studied the area, the only sound being the *drip, drip, drip* of water from the ceiling overhead. For a second time, the mark had mysteriously bolted from his hiding place. Strange behavior, to be sure. But the mark couldn't be far away. The lingering scent left behind by the man—the woman knew the mark was a "he" just from the smell—indicated that he wasn't long gone.

Eager to continue the search, the woman exited from the chill of the cave into the warm, humid night. Her eyes suddenly zeroed in on something moving through the underbrush. In a movement so swift it defied reality, she grabbed a rodent from the ground and stuffed it into her mouth. The rodent's tail was briefly visible, wagging in desperation, before the woman sucked it in like a strand of spaghetti.

The woman's midnight snack was not typical. The

approaching new moon—only two days from now—was what had caused the disgusting urge to chow down on a forest rat. The guttata always went a little off course this time of month. The hormones were jumpin', it was difficult to concentrate on much of anything, sleep was out of the question. So the spew-inducing, furry hors d'oeuvre the woman had just eaten—swallowing it whole in a single gulp—was simply an impulse. She couldn't help herself.

Besides, it gave her a hit of protein to fuel her ongoing and very promising search for the missing mark.

8

The morning after Toby had successfully pulled off a getaway to join Annabel for what turned out to be an uneventful stakeout, he stood in the driveway with his dad. Steam rose lazily from the asphalt drive, the early morning sun evaporating the moisture from the previous night's rainfall. Toby's mother, sister, and her young friend were already in the car, which idled at the curb.

"You have no idea how much convincing I had to do to sway your mother on this one, Toby. Especially after the incident at the hospital last night."

"I think I do. Thanks, Dad. I appreciate it."

"All I ask is that you earn my trust over the next week. No funny stuff. Deal?"

Toby nodded. His father gave him a pat on the shoulder, walked to the car, slid behind the wheel, and drove off down the street. Waving to his departing family, Toby felt guilty. Here he'd been doing one thing after another behind his parents' backs, and now he had promised his father there would be no "funny stuff" for the next week. Of course, there would be funny stuff! What particular variety, Toby didn't know, but that was practically all he'd been doing for the past month or so. Funny stuff.

All Toby could hope at this point was that his well-intentioned transgressions would be worth it, in the end.

■ ■ ■

That night it was Toby and Strobe's turn for the sunset-to-midnight stakeout shift. Earlier, an unusually tense Harvey had stressed how important it was to keep up the stakeouts, boring though they may be. The new moon was in less than twenty-four hours. If Chris Child didn't show up within that time frame, that was it. They would have to wait another month for a chance to follow him to the monthly Gathering.

That would give their foes a possibly unbeatable advantage in the treacherous cat-and-mouse game that was being waged between the two camps. That was the last thing Harvey wanted to give his enemies, so he was urging everyone to be on their toes.

The first hour of Toby and Strobe's stakeout was quiet as the two took turns with a pair of binoculars to study the Child house below. Toby had tried to engage Strobe in conversation a couple of times, but so far, no go.

"What's wrong, Strobe?" Toby asked after another silent half hour had gone by.

"Nothin'."

Toby knew that wasn't true. He could tell *something* was troubling his stakeout partner. He considered leaving the moody guy be, but wasn't sure if he could handle another hour and a half of silence.

"You're way too quiet for nothing to be wrong. C'mon. Talk to me. I'm your wingman, after all. Whatever you say goes no further than here."

Strobe stared at Child's house. From where they sat, they could see the living room, eerily illuminated by the bluish light of a large TV screen.

"Did you and Annabel talk much last night?"

Toby was surprised by Strobe's question. "During the stakeout, you mean?" Strobe nodded. "Yeah, of course we talked. Why?"

"Nothin'," Strobe said. "It's nothin'. Really."

"What do you mean, it's nothin'? It's *something*, or you wouldn't have brought it up."

"Forget it, Tobe." Strobe raised the binoculars to his eyes. He clearly was not interested in continuing the conversation.

Sitting cross-legged on the ground, Toby tapped his foot in frustration. "Know what? I don't want to forget it. I don't want to sit here quiet as a tree stump for the next hour and a half."

"So call Annabel."

"Know what I'm really talking about here? Having a simple conversation. What's wrong with that?"

"Nothing. But let me clue you in on something. Some guys don't like to gab all the time."

"Yeah, well, how 'bout *some* of the time? I mean, you don't like to gab, like . . . *ever*. Think about it. I've been working with you for practically two months and hardly know a thing about you. I don't even know where you live. Here we've trained together. Gone up against the guttata together. You gave me a *nickname*. It seems to me we should be able to just . . . talk, you know?"

Actually, Toby had a pretty good idea why Strobe had asked the question about whether or not he and Annabel had talked during their stakeout. Annabel had revealed to him the previous night that she and Strobe

187

hadn't talked much during their stakeout. Strobe had seemed distracted, Annabel thought. Uneasy.

Toby had a theory about why Strobe had been like that with Annabel. The guy had a crush on her. Toby was sure of it. Well, no surprise there. How could a guy *not* have a crush on Annabel? Toby certainly did. Of course he knew that Annabel only saw him as a friend, which had given him more than a few private little heartaches.

But yeah, Strobe had a thing for Annabel, that much was clear to Toby. The guy was so cool—most of the time, anyway—but Toby had noticed those glances he threw in Annabel's direction from time to time, especially after a particularly intense self-defense class. He was totally into her. Definitely.

"Know what?" Toby said, breaking the stillness in the small, cave-like chamber in the middle of the bushes. "I'm not gonna hound you about this conversation thing. But I need some coffee. I'll fall asleep just sitting here like this. Want anything at the Stop and Go?"

"No. Thanks."

Toby stood and started pushing his way through the bushes. Strobe lowered his binoculars, looked at Toby, then suddenly said, "Hidden Hills Suites."

Toby stopped and looked over his shoulder at Strobe. Hidden Hills Suites? What did that mean?

"That's where I live," Strobe explained. "Hidden Hills Suites. Down on Streets Run."

Toby knew where the Hidden Hills Suites were. It wasn't the most desirable place to live, that's for sure. Besides that, it was mainly for people and families who probably wouldn't be staying in Hidden Hills for very long.

"What else do you want to know?" Strobe asked.

Toby couldn't help but smile. "This isn't an interrogation, Strobe."

"No? It feels like one."

"Okay . . . Listen, I have an idea." Toby returned to his stakeout spot. "This might help. Why don't we take turns telling each other something about ourselves. That way it won't feel like you're my prisoner or something."

"In that case, it's your turn."

Toby looked surprised. "So . . . you actually want to do this?"

"Better get started before I change my mind."

"Right . . . right." Toby thought about what to tell Strobe about himself. After a few moments . . .

"Is it really that hard?" Strobe asked.

"I don't want to spout off the first thing that comes to mind. I want this back-and-forth to *mean* something."

Strobe rubbed his forehead as though he had a headache.

"I've lived in the same house my entire life," Toby finally revealed.

"I've moved more than five times in the last three years."

"Get out! Why do you move so much?"

"No questions. Your turn."

"Okay, right. No questions." After a moment . . . "I was in the Cub Scouts when I was little, but when I got to the Boy Scouts . . . I don't know. I just wasn't that into it. So I quit. I guess I'm not that much of a joiner, when you come right down to it."

"My mom works as a temporary restaurant manager. Comes in when they're starting things up, trains the people, then it's off to the next place after things are up and running. That's why I've moved so much."

"That's interesting. See, this isn't so bad, is it? We're actually conversing."

"Don't push it, Tobe."

"My turn, right?" Toby frowned in concentration,

thinking, then suddenly smiled. "This is a good one. I was around ten years old. I was playing baseball in the backyard. I had this whole thing worked out where I could play an entire game by myself. So anyway, I threw the ball against the wall and it went flying over my head and landed in my mom's flower garden. I went over to pick it up and this thin stake, my mom put it there for a vine to grow on or something, went right up my nose."

Strobe looked at Toby, deadpan.

"It was really bad. My dad had to take me to the emergency room. The stake had gone all the way up to my—"

"Hold it right there. I've heard enough about this one."

"Yeah, well . . . top *that*, huh?"

Strobe didn't hesitate. "When I was around nine, my dad and I were playing baseball behind our apartment building. He had a heart attack and died, right there in front of me."

Toby couldn't believe what Strobe had just told him. It was the absolute last thing he expected to hear.

"Actually, he didn't die right away. In the meantime, though, I just stood there like an idiot, staring at him."

Toby struggled for something to say. "I'm sure . . ."

"There wasn't anything I could do, right? That's what my mom always says." Strobe looked away, off into the darkness. "Anyway, that'll teach you to start up a conversation with me, huh? If we'd gone back and forth a few more times you might have found out how I spent half a year at a detention camp for stealing a car, among other things. When I was twelve."

Strobe looked at Toby, then nodded abruptly, indicating that this particular conversation was over. Toby sat in the darkness, at a loss for words. Strobe's revelations had been like a sharp jab to the stomach.

Demons.

The word just popped into Toby's head. There were the outer kind, of course, the kind they were fighting. Toby now knew Strobe had a few of the inner kind to deal with. Which explained a bit about why he was the way he was.

"You see that?!" Strobe suddenly asked. He was already grabbing his backpack.

Toby had seen it. He was too shocked to speak. A large figure had just darted across the backyard of the Child house. The figure didn't look human. Matter-of-fact, scurrying across the yard on all fours, it resembled the guttata hanging in the Killer Pizza classroom!

9

Toby and Strobe burst from their hiding place and ran down the hill toward the Child house. Toby lost his footing halfway down, rolled the rest of the way, and took out a few bushes before flopping to a stop at the edge of the backyard.

Strobe yanked Toby to his feet. The two stood shoulder to shoulder and scoured the now deserted yard, their hyper in-and-out breathing the only audible sound in the quiet night.

"That was a guttata," Strobe said as he yanked on his backpack.

"Couldn't have been Child, then. Harvey said he'd return in human form."

Strobe snapped down his NVGs and pulled his crossbow out of his backpack. "Let's go get it, whatever it was. I'll take the left side."

Toby started for the right side of the house as he pulled on his backpack. A high hedge separated the Child house from the house next door, creating a narrow alley along the length of the house to the front yard.

Toby walked cautiously down the deserted hedge-alley, staying close to the house as he watched for any sign of movement in the darkness ahead. He was snapping an arrow cartridge onto his crossbow, when—

Tap! Tap! Tap!

Toby jerked his head up to look at the roof, where he had heard the sound of pattering feet. He turned his back to the alley as he retreated to the backyard for a better look at the roof. *I hope Mrs. Child has those upstairs windows locked!*

Toby was almost to the backyard when a brittle rustling sound interrupted the silence in the alley behind him. He whirled around, then stumbled back in horror at the sight that greeted him. Something had just stepped from the shadows into a small pool of light that shone from a nearby window.

That something was "Chris Child."

Child's otherworldly transformation was almost complete. *Almost* being the operative word. His ears had almost disappeared into the sides of his hairless head. His enlarged chest jutted out weirdly from his deformed body. The long-fingered, lizard-like hands and feet were still partly human, the old, flesh-colored skin stretched over a new, alien system of bones and ligaments.

But it was mainly the *face* that held Toby's horrified attention. It was as though Child's face had been pulled and molded to fit the contour of an elongated guttata face. His remaining facial features were a grotesque, fun-house-mirror-like parody of what Child used to look like.

The guttata in the woods had been terrifying to Toby, but this specimen was *beyond* terrifying. Child was something that simply *shouldn't be*.

As Toby backed away, the freakish-looking creature skittered awkwardly toward him on all fours, looking like what he was. A human—*former* human—trying to adjust to a strange new way of walking. Fortunately for Toby, Child was still human-size and not yet at full guttata strength. Just the same, Toby wanted to avoid a tussle with the thing if he could help it. He raised his crossbow to his shoulder to discourage Child from coming any closer. The creature responded by rearing back and contorting his features in a frightening grimace.

Strike pose!

Toby had no choice. He took aim and fired. The arrow pierced Child's shoulder, causing him to cry out as he fell back. Quickly regaining his balance, Child snarled at Toby, a look of rage inflaming his black-red eyes. Then he charged!

Hisssss! Thunk!

The crossbow arrow—looking as though it had materialized out of thin air and was now imbedded in the grass between Child's feet—stopped Child in his tracks. The hybrid's head twisted like an owl's and looked up at the roof.

Toby glanced up and saw Strobe at roof's edge, a darker silhouette against the dark, starless night sky. He was readying his bow for another shot. When Toby focused back on the ground in front of him . . .

Child was no longer there.

A residual shaking of branches in the nearby hedge indicated which way the creature had gone. Toby looked up to see Strobe take aim with his crossbow. But he pulled up before firing. He looked down at Toby and shook his head no.

Child had escaped into the night.

■ ■ ■

An impromptu meeting was held in Harvey's Jeepster Commando—his official "field car"—which Harvey had parked down the street from the Child house. Harvey, Steve, and Annabel had joined Toby and Strobe within ten minutes after receiving their call.

"What do you think Child will do now?" Annabel asked.

"Anybody's guess," Harvey said. "Coming home before completing his transformation? Definitely abnormal." The normally deadpan, cool-as-ice Harvey was clearly disturbed at this latest development.

"I think he'll return to his hideout," Steve suggested. "A family reunion certainly didn't work out for him. If that's what he was after."

"Doubtful he'll come back here tonight, in any case," Harvey said. "Just the same, I'll take my usual shift. You three go home. Get a good night's rest."

End of meeting. Strobe opened the rear door of the Jeepster and he, Annabel, and Toby hopped out.

"Where do you think you're going?" Steve said. "Get back in here. We'll give you a lift home."

"I'm cool," Strobe said.

"I'm just around the corner," Annabel said.

"Sure?"

The trio nodded.

"All right. Just be sure to keep a watch out for other guttata. They might be hovering about."

The trio waved to the Commando as it moved off down the street, then were silent after the car had disappeared around the corner.

"Interesting evening." It was Strobe who broke the silence.

Annabel looked at Strobe and Toby. "You two did good. Who knows what might have happened to Mrs. Child if . . . well, you know."

Toby and Strobe knew.

"Either of you want a ride?" Annabel asked as she walked across the street to get her bike.

"No, thanks," Strobe said.

"Toby?"

"I don't have that far to go, Annabel. I'm gonna walk with Strobe."

"Okay. See you tomorrow. Be careful." Strobe and Toby waved to Annabel as she hopped onto her bike and rode off, then headed in the opposite direction from which she had gone. They were quiet as they walked down the middle of the deserted street.

"See ya," Strobe said when they arrived at the first

intersection. He turned left and started up the steep road that crisscrossed Finney Drive.

"Strobe?" Toby said. Strobe turned and looked at Toby as he continued walking, backward, up the hill. "You had my back tonight. Thanks."

"What are friends for?"

Toby stood in the middle of the intersection and watched Strobe until he had passed beyond the light of a streetlamp and was out of sight. The quiet moment was rudely interrupted by the blast of a car horn behind Toby.

Toby jumped out of the way as a BMW stuffed with guys and girls roared past him.

"Outta the way, you deek!" someone yelled from the car. Toby shook his head at the sight of the car, burning rubber as it sped up the steep road.

"To protect and serve," he said. Then he headed home.

10

After his explosive run-in with Chris Child, Toby decided the only thing to do was hit the kitchen.

Tonight of all crazy nights might not appear to be the best time for Toby to get flour-dusty in the kitchen, but he knew he had to do *something*. He wouldn't be able to fall asleep any time soon, that was for sure. A kitchen session just might help him calm down a bit.

Besides, Toby had been wanting to try out a couple of ideas for two new KP pizzas, two original recipes he would present to Harvey, if and when they turned out the way he hoped they would.

One of his recipes had been inspired by a Saturday morning pancake breakfast his mom had recently cooked up for the family. Reaching for the syrup that morning, Toby had suddenly thought . . . *Syrup. Pizza. A sweet pizza. A breakfast pizza!*

As for the other recipe—a spicy, deep-dish number—Toby already had a name for that one: Dragon Breath!

All of the items on Killer Pizza's menu had fun, cartoon figures next to them, appropriate to each name. In his mind's eye, Toby could already picture the fire-breathing dragon next to Dragon Breath.

The bottom line? Toby knew he had to branch out at some point. Invent something new. Any serious chef had to do that, and Toby still had designs on becoming a serious chef. One of these days.

So Toby got busy. The time flew by—and Toby's hyper state gradually dissipated—as he rolled out the dough for his two pizza pies and prepared his own special sauces. He felt like a conductor as he cut his fruit and vegetables, and the delicious-smelling sweet and spicy sauces bubbled in their saucepans. The kitchen was his stage! The spatula his baton!

However, when Toby tasted his two new KP pizzas, he was disappointed. The various flavors in his Dragon Breath pizza seemed to be competing instead of complementing one another. As for the breakfast pizza . . . well, that one needed *a lot* of work.

The failure of Toby's two creations caused his always lurking insecurities to rise to the surface. It was one thing to simply take an existing recipe and re-create it in the kitchen, which is what Toby had been doing ever since he started at Killer Pizza. It was clearly another—and more difficult—thing to come up with one's own recipes.

You'll just have to try again, a weary Toby thought as he put the perishables in the refrigerator. But "try again" would have to wait. Toby was through for the evening. Exhaustion had overtaken him. So, after *not* cleaning up the rest of the mess in the kitchen (a no-no when his mom was around), Toby stretched out on the living room sofa in his boxers (another no-no) and surfed the channels. He needed to zone out on a movie. Something fun.

He found just the thing on one of the pay channels, a goofy 1950s camp classic called *Invasion of the Saucer Men*. Aliens (with alcohol for blood!) battling hot-rodding teens. How could you go wrong with that scenario?

But as wonderfully bad as the movie was, it was no match for Toby's fatigue. An amputated alien hand was crawling toward two teens on Lover's Lane when Toby's eyelids slowly closed . . . and he fell into a deep sleep.

Toby woke instantly.

There was none of that half-awake, hazy coming-to after a deep sleep. No, this was definitely different.

Toby was *awake*.

Still lying on the living room sofa.

Staring at the TV.

Listening for a return of the sound that woke him.

The *skittering* sound.

Except for the TV, there were no other lights on in the living room. Toby glanced around the empty, silent room.

Maybe the sound was in my dream.

Toby had dreamed again. As before, it had been the terrifying Alpha nightmare. But this time, Toby had awoken *before* the Alpha gripped his shoulder. Which had made the dream even more disturbing somehow.

But that was probably it, Toby figured. The distinctive skittering sound had actually been the Alpha's churning wings in his dream. Toby allowed himself to relax. The thought occurred to him that he should probably go up to his bedroom. On the other hand, it was so nice and comfy on the sofa. . . .

Skit! Skit! Skit!

Toby's nervous system exploded. He sat bolt upright and stared into the darkness. The sound had come from the dark corner behind the TV. Toby's mind was racing but his muscles felt frozen, locked in place. It gave him the strange sensation of traveling very fast while sitting perfectly still. As he sat glued to the sofa, he watched the *silhouette of a head* slowly appear over the top of the TV. It was a strangely distorted head. Totally *wrong*. If Toby had been freaked at Child's house, what he felt now could properly be described as *catatonic*.

Here he was, sitting in his boxers in his living room . . .

. . . staring into the glaring black-red eyes of Chris Child.

11

He followed me home!

Toby had time for that one panicked thought before Child vaulted over the top of the TV and charged him like a guttata linebacker! Shoving as hard as he could with his legs, Toby flipped the sofa over backward.

BAMMMM!!!!

The sofa shuddered as Child slammed into the suddenly exposed bottom of the couch. Toby executed a somersault away from the sofa and leaped to his feet. The creature clawed over the sofa, eyes blazing red-hot.

Toby ran to the fireplace, grabbed the poker from its stand, and held it out in front of him like a sword. Child skidded to a stop less than ten feet from Toby and retreated slightly.

Standoff.

It didn't last long. The creature sensed Toby's fear,

and that's all it needed to resume the attack. Circling around Toby, it charged, the still slightly human mouth opening wide to reveal very inhuman-like fangs.

Toby yanked the shovel from the fireplace stand and smacked Child across the face with it. He followed up with a poker-jab into the creature's gut, piercing the soft underbelly. Child cried out in pain and fell back.

"Yeah! How do you like *that*, huh?" Toby was suddenly livid at the bizarre-looking hybrid that had invaded the sanctity of his home. His *home*!

But anger couldn't overcome Toby's concern about how to get out of his desperate situation. Suddenly feeling the cold bricks of the fireplace against his bare legs, he took a sideways step to put more distance between him and the stalking creature.

Oh, no! Toby thought frantically when his foot caught on the floor-level fireplace gas lever. Unable to stay upright, Toby fell to the floor with a thud. Child hissed and skittered toward him!

GAS! FIRE!

The thought hit Toby like a punch. He threw his shovel at Child to create a split-second diversion, then reached out and twisted the gas lever as far as it would go. Fire burst from the fake logs. The creature immediately leaped back, panic and surprise showing in its eyes.

"HA!" Toby yelled. Pulling himself to his feet, he couldn't help but smile at the creature. But Toby's sense of triumph was short-lived. The fire wouldn't keep Child at bay for long. Toby felt panic starting to rise up from his gut, an overpowering sensation that threatened to quickly consume him, render him helpless. He struggled to stay in control of his emotions. But he was losing it. He could feel all control slipping away!

Toby desperately looked around the room for a way out. Child was preparing for another charge, he could tell.

The kitchen! Toby suddenly thought.

The kitchen was on the other side of the room from where Toby stood. But that's where Toby knew he had to go. Tons of weapons in the kitchen. Knives. Frying pans. Plenty of lethal things to work with.

But how to get past Child?

Toby suddenly had the answer.

He threw his last weapon—the poker—at the creature, then grabbed a nearby lamp and stuck it shade-first into the fire.

WHOOOOOSH!!! The lamp shade immediately caught fire.

Toby jabbed the lamp at Child. Enraged, the hybrid snarled and hissed, but retreated backward. Toby moved toward one side of the living room, all the while holding the burning lamp protectively out in front of him. He needed to get *around* Child, instead of just backing him up toward the kitchen. He was halfway toward his destination when—

POP!!!!

The lamp's lightbulb exploded from the heat!

Toby dropped the lamp in surprise. The creature leaped back from the explosion. The lamp shade flame fizzled and went out.

And then . . .

Silence. Toby stared at Child. Child stared back at Toby. A very human expression suddenly flashed in the creature's eyes. It knew it *had* Toby. He was totally vulnerable. Away from the fire in the corner of the room. No poker for a weapon. No flaming lamp shade.

MOVE OR DIE!!!!!

Those three words zapped Toby into action just as the creature charged. He grabbed the lamp from the floor and rammed its smoking end into Child's open, snarling mouth. Then he ran like hell for the kitchen!

Child spit out the lamp shade and leaped after Toby.

Caught from behind, Toby felt his legs go out from under him. Reaching out wildly for something to break his fall, he pulled a small end table down with him instead as he slammed to the floor.

The creature yanked Toby around, pinned him with one powerful hand on his chest, and opened its ravenous, saliva-dripping mouth.

Toby reached out and grasped Child's neck in a desperate attempt to hold the creature's head—and those glinting, pointed teeth—as far away from his body as possible. But Toby couldn't match Child's superior strength. The creature's head moved closer and closer to Toby's neck. Toby gasped from the strain of trying to keep Child at bay. His muscles were giving out. He couldn't hold off the creature much longer! But then—

Bong . . . Bong . . . Bong . . .

The creature's head swiveled toward the living room grandfather clock, chiming the midnight hour.

A reprieve! Toby grabbed a heavy metal sculpture of a cowboy on the back of a rearing horse, which had fallen from the end table, and smacked Child across the side of the head with all the strength he could muster.

The hybrid's eyes glazed over as it fell to one side.

Toby struggled to get out from under the creature and pulled himself to his feet. He leaped over a nearby recliner and sprinted across the living room.

Quickly shaking off Toby's blow, the creature whirled and pushed off with its powerful legs. It was a deadly footrace to the kitchen!

Toby grabbed a post at the corner of the counter that separated the kitchen from the living room. He swung himself around just as Child vaulted toward him.

Toby slammed into the counter from the centrifugal force of his swing. Child flew past him and skidded across the linoleum floor.

Toby quickly scanned the kitchen counter. He grabbed one of the pizza pans and held it up in front of him like a shield as the creature shoved off from the base of the oven and flung itself across the kitchen.

CRACKKKKKK!!!

The force of the creature's attack bent the pan in half. Pizza slices flew everywhere!

With a strong shove, Toby forced Child back to the center of the narrow kitchen, then snatched his Mario Rocco pizza slicer with the polycarbonate wheel ($12.41, Toby had discovered, when ordered from the Rocco Web site) from the counter.

The creature propelled itself back at Toby. Toby spun around 360 degrees, narrowly avoiding razor-sharp, snarling fangs, and slashed the creature's shoulder with his pizza slicer.

Child squealed in pain. Toby grabbed a jar of red chili powder (not the best choice for his Dragon Breath pizza, Toby had to admit) and flung the entire contents into the creature's face. The hybrid roared and clawed at its stinging, burning eyes.

Taking a quick inventory of kitchen utensils, Toby tossed the pizza wheel and chili jar aside and reached for the portable hand mixer. As he yanked the mixer cord from the outlet, his elbow jerked and hit the bowl of leftover pizza dough, knocking it to the floor.

CRASH!

Before the flailing creature could regain its sight—and advantage in the life-and-death struggle—Toby quickly got behind the hybrid, wrapped the mixer cord around its neck, and started to drag it from the kitchen.

The creature reacted violently, blindly lashing out with its talons. A long, razor-sharp toe talon found its mark and slashed a wide cut across Toby's thigh. Toby winced from the pain but managed to hold on to the creature. He pulled it backward into the short hallway that led to the basement.

Child slashed and kicked. . . . Toby desperately tried to gain traction on the greasy, pizza-strewn, dough-covered linoleum floor with his bare feet. . . . The hybrid grabbed at the cord that was cutting off its air. . . . Toby muscled the struggling creature ever closer to the basement door. . . .

It was a strange-looking dance of flailing limbs and stutter-step motion. Blinking away streams of sweat that ran into his eyes, Toby reached out with one hand, grabbed the basement doorknob, and flung the door open.

Using the mixer cord like a slingshot, he mustered up his last bit of energy, swung the hybrid around, and sent it flying down the basement steps. The creature disappeared into the darkness of the cellar with a series of thuds and ungodly screeches. Toby quickly slammed the door and locked it.

Fighting back the impulse to collapse to the hallway floor, Toby limped back to the kitchen and grabbed the phone. As he punched in a number, a talon burst through the wooden basement door!

"Harvey here," came the voice over the phone.

"Harvey!" Toby yelled in a hoarse whisper, his voice having suddenly disappeared on him for some reason. "Child followed me home!"

"Hold tight. We're on our way."

Suddenly, an entire *handful* of talons sliced through the basement door, rocketing splinters across the hall-way.

"Better hurry," Toby urged. "He's *really upset!*"

12

Harvey and Steve arrived to find Toby sitting slack-
jawed on the piano bench in the living room, surveying
the damage as the creature steadily battered away at
the basement door.

"He . . . just . . . won't . . . *give up!*"

Toby had managed to pound a patchwork of two-
by-fours across the frame of the basement door. Good
thing, too. Even with the door reinforced, the creature
had shredded it and was about to break free of its
prison.

Harvey and Steve snapped into action. Steve stitched
up Toby's wound as Harvey fired a sedative dart into
Child's neck through the disintegrated basement door.
The Commando was backed into the garage and the now
slumbering fiend was retrieved from the basement floor
and loaded into the Jeepster's trunk.

Once all that was done, Harvey and Steve returned to the living room. Toby hadn't moved from the piano bench.

"I'll have a crew in here first thing tomorrow to clean this up," Harvey said. "They'll replace whatever was damaged. It'll look good as new when they're done."

Toby was glad to hear that. That just might get him out of being grounded for the rest of his life. Harvey looked at Toby for a moment, then sat on the bench next to him. "So . . . talk to me. How are you feeling?"

Toby thought about the question. "Lucky to be alive."

Harvey shook his head. "Luck has nothing to do with it. You took the skills we taught you and used them in the field. The bottom line, Toby? You found some of that inner strength I was talking about. I'm very impressed."

"So am I," Steve added. "It's incredible you were able to fight that creature off."

High praise from Harvey and Steve. And Harvey was right, Toby realized. Somehow or other he had managed to reach down and find some of that inner strength when he needed it most.

"Did you finish Child off?" Toby suddenly asked.

Harvey didn't answer for a moment, then said, "No."

"Why not?"

"I need to study him," Harvey said. "Then I'll send him to New York for more tests. I'm always looking for techniques, drugs, to bring these creatures back. Given the choice, I believe any hybrid would want to return to the human community. Imperfect as we are."

That made Toby think about Chelsea, lying helplessly in the hospital.

"You're coming with us tonight," Harvey said, rising from the bench. "No way do I want you here alone."

Toby didn't argue. He gave his trashed living room a final look, then followed Harvey and Steve into the garage and got into the Commando. Completely spent from his battle with Child, he was asleep before Harvey had even backed the car out onto the street.

■ ■ ■

As the Jeepster moved off down Hazel Street, a dark figure appeared from the woods behind Toby's house. Dressed in black, the figure moved to Toby's side yard just in time to see the Commando's rear lights disappear down the street.

The blue-eyed woman had finally tracked down her mark. She took out her cell phone, had a brief conversation, then walked up Toby's driveway. She hesitated a moment in the middle of the deserted street, her translucent eyes coldly reflecting the glow of the moon sliver overhead, then started down the hill, toward Killer Pizza.

The cat-and-mouse game was over.

It was time for war.

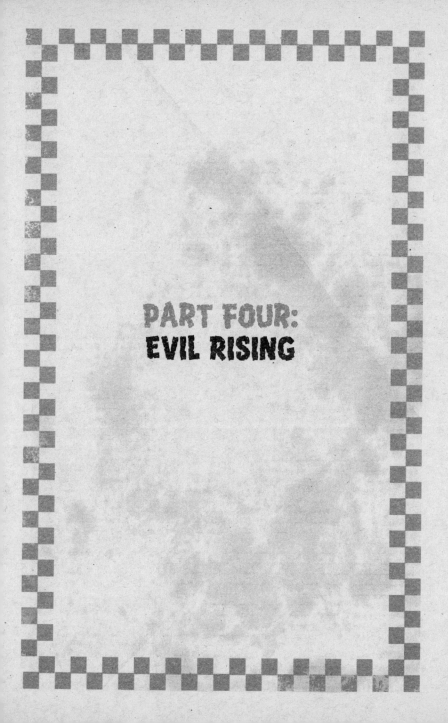

PART FOUR:
EVIL RISING

1

Harvey was in the autopsy/forensics room, studying a sample of Child's blood when he heard the sound. Steve had gone home earlier at Harvey's insistence. Toby was asleep on a cot in the classroom. It was past two in the morning.

The sound had come from one of the security TV monitors in Harvey's basement office, monitors that relayed images from the pizza shop, upstairs office, storage room, and back alley. When Harvey walked into his office he literally got goose bumps from what he saw on one of the monitors. Two hooded people had broken into Killer Pizza!

One man—burly, large forearms—and one woman were on the pizza shop screen, prowling about in the kitchen. Harvey's first thought was, how did they manage to get in without setting off the alarm? He didn't have a clue, but he did know the two intruders were guttata. They had that look about them. Even in human form, guttata had a certain way of walking. Slow, assured, no unnecessary movements, as though to preserve their strength for more important things.

But were there just two of them? Harvey checked the screen that scanned the back alley. The monitor showed two large, hulking black vehicles. A cluster of figures—just their dark shapes visible—stood in the shadows near the SUVs.

Okay, Harvey thought. *Game's on.* He was calm and composed as he took out his cell phone and called Steve. Steve was to come to Killer Pizza immediately. He was to park on Hazel Street, fifty yards from the Industrial Avenue turnoff, and wait until he saw a black Hummer and a black Yukon appear from the dead-end street. He was to follow the Hummer. Wherever it went, Steve must not let it out of his sight. Steve said he'd be there in five minutes.

"Make it four," Harvey replied.

Four minutes later the two human guttata were in the storage room, ripping it apart in an attempt to find some indication of where Child had been taken. Harvey called Steve to make sure he was in place, then tapped a few numbers into the phone after Steve hung up.

The alarm for the KP building started to blare. The guttata had been clever enough to get into KP without tripping the main alarm, but they couldn't do anything about the backup system, which Harvey had activated with his cell.

The intruders stopped in their tracks. Harvey watched them hesitate, then slowly retreat from the storage room to the pizza shop, and finally to the back alley.

Ten figures huddled in the darkness before getting into the SUVs. When the large vehicles moved off down the alley and disappeared from sight, Harvey nodded. Just like that, he had countered the guttata's first move.

"Why's the alarm on?" Toby asked from the doorway, shielding his eyes from the bright light in the office.

"Everything's fine," Harvey replied. "Go back to sleep."

"But . . ." Toby suddenly noticed the trashed storage room on the monitor. "Uh-oh. Is that what I think it is?"

"Yes. They've found us. But we . . . are about to find them."

2

"It's about time! What are we waiting for? Let's go get 'em!"

Strobe, along with Annabel, had just received the news that Steve was currently staking out a house in Brentwood Hills, where the black Hummer had immediately gone after the alarm went off. It was now afternoon and the driver—the burly man who had broken into Killer Pizza—had not reappeared from the house since going inside the previous night.

As for the rest of the guttata, they had scattered and driven off into the night and were now waiting somewhere in the city for the Gathering to begin. Which is right where the burly man would lead them, come nightfall.

"I've done a background check on this man," Harvey said. "His name is Thomas Gome. He's second-in-command in the Brentwood Hills Police Department."

Strobe whistled through his teeth. "They do have people in high places, don't they?"

Harvey nodded. "I've called headquarters. Reinforcements will be here any time now."

Strobe frowned at this news. "Reinforcements? What are you talking about?"

"Ten of KP's best officers are coming in from New York."

"Wait a second. You're not saying we're being replaced, are you?"

"I am. You will not be going out in the field with us tonight, Strobe."

"But this is *our* case."

"It's too dangerous. I need my most experienced officers on this one."

"We're experienced. We took on those guttata."

"Yes, you did. But they were child's play compared to an Alpha."

"I know I'm ready for this, Harvey."

"And I know you're not. You're still a rookie, after all. The people coming in have completed their advanced training in New York. They have years of experience in the field."

"Advanced training in New York? You never mentioned anything about advanced training in New York."

"That's because you haven't even finished your initial training here in Hidden Hills."

"What's with this advanced training? What more could you teach us?"

"Let's just say that what you're into here is like trying out for a police force. Advanced training is the equivalent of trying out for the CIA."

Intriguing . . .

"Wait. . . . I get it. You've been planning this all along, haven't you? We do the preliminary, boring stakeout work, then you call in the big boys."

"You'll get your shot, Strobe. Now's not the time. But I do think you should hang around. Meet the officers. Steve and a few of them will be monitoring the situation from my office tonight while we're out in the field. It'd be a good thing for you to observe."

"No way am I sitting here like some little kid while the big boys are off having all the fun." With that, Strobe brushed past Harvey on his way out of the office. Annabel gave Harvey an apologetic shrug.

"He's just a really gung-ho kind of guy."

"And bullheaded. It'll be a while before the troops arrive and things get going. You can stick around here if you want. If not, keep an eye out. See you around six o'clock." With that, Harvey turned and walked out of his office.

Toby and Annabel were silent after Harvey left, each with their own thoughts. Annabel didn't love the idea of being replaced by more experienced officers, either. She was surprised how strongly she felt about that. She could have never guessed how eager an officer she would become when she first signed up for the MCO Academy.

As for Toby, he didn't mind the "big boys" coming in and taking over. Not after what he'd just been through. Matter-of-fact, Toby was looking forward to taking in the action from Harvey's office. It'd be like observing a football game from the announcer's booth. Nice and safe, with no chance of getting your head bashed in.

3

Strobe sat in an abandoned forklift in the littered field at the end of Industrial Avenue, keeping a watch on Killer Pizza. He was waiting for the KP troops to arrive. He couldn't help himself. He was intensely curious about Harvey's veteran MCOs. What would they look like? Would their experience show in their faces? In the way they moved? Strobe knew he had to find out.

So, unlike Toby and Annabel, who had gone home for a few hours until things got going later in the afternoon, Strobe waited in the heat of the afternoon until he saw two black sedans appear at the end of the street. As they disappeared into the alley that ran behind the buildings on the right side of the avenue, Strobe hopped from the forklift and headed for Killer Pizza.

Pushing through the front door, Strobe walked under a banner that had recently been strung across the shop.

The banner referred to the all-night horror movie marathon parties that some teens had begun having around Hidden Hills. Ever the smart businessman, Harvey immediately installed the banner when word got back to him about the parties. He especially liked the part where the kids ordered plenty of Killer Pizzas and side dishes before settling in for their dusk-till-dawn screamfests. To extract as much money from the kids as possible, Harvey had stocked several shelves with classic horror films by the take-out counter as part of the "All-Nighter" package.

I'm about to have a horror party myself, Strobe thought as he swung over the counter and entered the kitchen. The new trio of pizza chefs Harvey had recently hired was buzzing wildly around the kitchen. It was five o'clock, the beginning of the busy dinner hours. Strobe was about to head down the hall to the storage room when the counter phone rang.

"Strobe! Can you get that?"

Everyone working "aboveground" thought Strobe, Toby, and Annabel were assistant managers for KP. It allowed the trio to come and go without suspicion. But it also allowed the kitchen workers to ask for help from the trio from time to time.

"Please?" the girl with the disheveled hairnet implored Strobe as the phone continued to ring.

Strobe reluctantly retreated back to the phone. "Killer Pizza . . . Uh-huh . . . Right . . . You want any Mummy Wraps with that? Vampire Stakes? . . . You got it. It'll be there in half an hour."

"Forty-five minutes!" the girl yelled from the kitchen.

"Forty-five minutes," Strobe said, correcting himself. He was placing the order on the wheel in the kitchen when the phone started up again.

"Don't even think about it!" Strobe said.

"C'mon, Strobe! We need some help here!"

"Talk to Harvey about that."

"We have. Besides, what're you doing right now that's so important?"

"Saving our fair city from imminent destruction."

The girl was not amused at Strobe's comeback. Strobe smiled, exited the kitchen, went down the hall, and entered the storeroom, which he and Toby and Annabel had helped restore to order after the invasion the night before. He opened the secret pizza-sauce door and closed it firmly behind him.

Walking down the spiral staircase, Strobe was surprised to see that the Killer Pizza basement was already a beehive of activity, Harvey's reinforcements having wasted no time gearing up for the looming battle.

Several of the officers were assembling, checking, and lining up artillery on the two examination tables in the forensics room.

Several more MCOs walked briskly into Harvey's office . . .

. . . just as two other black-T-shirt-clad officers came out, gesturing to each other as they talked.

The young men and women—early to mid-twenties, Strobe guessed—were focused and intense as they went about their business. They definitely carried an aura of experience, of confidence, about them. Strobe was instantly jealous. He wanted to be part of this group. Wanted to feel what it felt like, having so much "out in the field" experience.

An odd thought suddenly hit Strobe. He wondered if all of the officers gathered in the KP basement had put in their time at Killer Pizza—had twirled the dough in hot kitchens—before being tapped for the KP program.

Pizza and monsters. From the very beginning, a very odd and unexpected mix.

The distracting thought evaporated as Strobe focused on the two officers who were assembling the weapons.

"You one of the rookies?" the officer nearest Strobe

asked. Strobe didn't like the guy's tone, but he nodded in reply. "Look pretty young. Just stay out of our way and maybe we'll let you stick around."

Strobe felt his temper flare, like it was an actual thing inside his body, with a fuse. It took all his willpower to harness his anger and not go at the guy with the slightly long, shaggy hair. That's what the dude probably wanted, Strobe figured. Lay the "rookie" out. Show him who was boss.

So instead of confronting the muscled officer, Strobe walked past him to Harvey's office, stood outside the door, and eavesdropped on the activity inside.

He had arrived just in time. A cluster of MCOs was gathered around Harvey's desk, watching a GPS-equipped monitor that was focused on Brentwood Hills. A blinking blue light—representing Thomas Gome's Hummer, which Steve had bugged during the night—was moving slowly along the twisting streets of Hidden Hills' neighboring community.

Strobe felt his heart rate jump a few notches. Gome was off to the Gathering! Very soon, Killer Pizza would know the location of the Alpha's "lair." Then, come nightfall—the Gathering officially beginning at sunset—the siege would begin.

Strobe felt worse than ever that he was not going to be a part of it.

■ ■ ■

As Harvey instructed several of his officers to take one of the KP vehicles and put a tail on Gome, Annabel was sitting at her kitchen table and having something to eat before heading back to Killer Pizza. Actually, Annabel was only picking at her food as she stared out the window at the backyard, where the large pool reflected the late afternoon summer sun, breaking it into thousands of glittering pieces. She was too excited, thinking about the coming evening, to really concentrate on her meal.

The rest of the house was quiet. Annabel's dad was still at work, her mother off shopping somewhere. Fossie, the Oshiros' live-in maid, was usually around, but this was her day off.

The sparkling pool suddenly went dull, the result of a bank of clouds bullying into view on the horizon and blotting out the sun. At the same time, the front doorbell rang. Annabel slid off her chair, went to the door, and opened it. Two men were standing on the front porch. They both wore suits and sunglasses.

"Hello," said the taller man. "We're collecting

signatures for a resolution to halt development along Turtle Creek."

"Did you know that there is more pollution—"

"I can't sign that, can I?" Annabel asked, interrupting the second man. "I'm only fourteen."

"Are your parents home?"

That gave Annabel pause. She didn't want to tell these guys that she was home alone. Come to think of it, she really didn't like the look of either of them. They gave her the creeps.

"Yes, my father is. I'll go get him."

Annabel gave the men a smile, then slammed the door in their faces! It was just a gut feeling, but Annabel had the unnerving notion that the two men standing on her front porch were guttata!

Her immediate thought was to call Harvey. As she spun away from the front door . . .

. . . she came face-to-face with the luminous blue-eyed woman.

A flash of white. An instant of intense pain. Then Annabel collapsed to the tile floor, unconscious.

4

Unaware of what had happened to Annabel, Toby grabbed the house keys from the hook next to the kitchen phone and stuffed them in his pocket.

"I need to get back to Killer Pizza, guys. Be sure to lock up when you leave, okay?"

Toby had biked home to check up on the two workers Harvey had sent to repair the damages in his house. They were almost done replacing the basement door that Child had obliterated. Considering what was going on down at Killer Pizza, fixing up the mess in the house didn't seem quite as important to Toby. But of course it had to be done, and quickly. His parents were due home in a couple of days. After asking when the new sofa would be arriving—any day now was the reply—Toby headed for the garage.

He was gingerly getting on his bike—his leg still

hurt from the talon slash—when Strobe ran into view at the end of the driveway. Seeing Toby, he ran toward the garage and pulled the door shut behind him after entering.

"What's goin' on?" Toby asked, clearly perplexed at Strobe's sudden appearance, not to mention the fact that he was carrying several backpacks and had a long, hefty circular aluminum tube strapped across his back.

Strobe couldn't talk. He had run all the way from Killer Pizza in the hot sun and couldn't catch his breath. Toby went into the house and got a glass of water. After draining it in a single gulp, Strobe was finally able to say—

"They got our girl."

◾ ◾ ◾

It wasn't long after Gome had started for the Gathering, Strobe revealed, and Harvey had sent his two men to tail him, when the call came into Killer Pizza. It was the pack's head honcho.

Alpha Man.

The leader of the pack's demands were simple. If Harvey didn't back off, he'd never see Annabel again. If the guttata were left alone to have their Gathering in peace, she would be returned safe and sound to Killer

236

Pizza the following morning. Not only that, but the pack would disappear from the city. Never to be heard from again.

Toby felt light-headed after hearing this. Annabel, kidnapped! How could this have happened? Strobe knocked Toby back into the here and now with his declaration that the two of them were going to go and get Annabel.

"What?" Toby asked. "What was that, again?"

"We're gonna track Annabel down and get her back."

"What are you talking about?"

"What's not to understand? We're gonna find out where she is and go rescue her."

"Does Harvey know we're doing this?"

"No."

"I'm confused. Rescuing Annabel is Harvey territory, isn't it?"

"Did you hear a word of what I just told you? Harvey has to go along with the Alpha's demands. His hands are tied, man. The place is like a tomb down there. The Killer Pizza building is being watched, for sure. But *us*, you think any of those monsters will be watching us? Two teenagers? What harm could we possibly be?"

"Just the question I was about to ask."

"C'mon, Tobe. Don't let me down here."

"Back up a second, Strobe. Who's to say this guy won't keep his promise? Maybe Annabel will be returned tomorrow morning. We could mess up the whole deal, going after her."

"Look me in the eye and tell me you actually think some gargoyle psycho dude is gonna keep his word."

"I can look you in the eye and say . . . I don't know."

"Are you afraid to do this, Tobe?"

Strobe's question caught Toby off guard. He cleared his throat. Checked the stitches on his thigh.

"Don't worry about it. So am I."

Toby wasn't sure if he heard Strobe correctly.

"Only a fool wouldn't be," Strobe continued. "I mean, are you kidding? Going after one of the most feared fiends in the monster universe? A thing that stands more than ten feet tall and can snap your neck like a toothpick?"

"Correct me if I'm wrong, Strobe, but I thought you were trying to *convince* me to join you on this impossible mission."

"I am. Listen to me. This is important. You listening?"

Toby nodded. He was all ears.

"Even if Harvey and his gang were able to go after

Annabel, do you know why you and I have a better chance at saving her than they do?"

"No, I don't."

"Because we care more about her, that's why. When Harvey's done with us here? Whether or not we become MCOs? He's gone, man. So is Steve. It's sayonara. They're gonna be off to train some other low-paid rookies to fight monsters. But that's okay. You know why?"

Toby shook his head no.

"'Cause we're a team, man. We gotta go get one of our team back."

Toby felt a surge of pride when Strobe said that. He *was* a part of this team.

"I'm goin' even if you don't come with me," Strobe said. "If it's the last thing I do, I'm gonna go save Annabel."

Save Annabel.

Toby suddenly had a feeling about something, about the real *underneath* reason why Strobe had such fire in his eyes, why he would stop at nothing to get to Annabel. No way was Strobe going to stand idly by when someone so desperately needed his help. Not this time.

"Okay, Strobe," Toby heard himself saying. "Let's go get her."

Strobe gave Toby a nod, a look of appreciation showing in his eyes. Then he turned and opened the garage door, ready to take on the guttata army. Before doing that, however, he looked back over his shoulder at Toby.

"I think we're gonna have to take your bike."

5

Annabel was slowly regaining consciousness.

Sounds and sensations floated through her brain, went away, came back again.

She was on the floor of a vehicle with a powerful motor humming behind her. She was blindfolded and gagged, her hands tied behind her, her ankles bound together.

One sensation that wouldn't go away was the throbbing in her head. Man, did that hurt. Annabel forced herself to take deep breaths. She knew she needed to get past the pain and focus on what she might be able to do to get out of her predicament.

First, Annabel tested the ropes that bound her. Every one of them was so tight it bit into her skin. Just moving was painful.

Only the wrist ropes, then. *Keep things simple*, Annabel

counseled herself. By concentrating on the wrist ropes, and nothing else, Annabel thought maybe—just maybe—she would be able to get free before arriving wherever it was she was being taken.

If not . . . well, it would give her something to do in the meantime besides just freaking out, which is what she really felt like doing.

■ ■ ■

Back at Killer Pizza, the mood was as downbeat as it could possibly be. The troops were gathered in the locker room and gym, waiting for further word on the guttata.

Harvey was holed up in his office. Nobody had seen him since he had called off the tail on Gome. That had been more than an hour ago. Since then, Gome had exchanged his Hummer for a "clean" vehicle—the guttata obviously suspected that Gome's SUV was bugged—which meant that Harvey's tracking screen was of no further use. With no tail on Gome, and no tracking device in his vehicle, the location of the Alpha's home would remain a mystery.

Steve knew how tough it had been for Harvey to give in to the Alpha's demands. Doing that meant the guttata would win this battle. At the same time, there was no guarantee any of the Alpha's promises would be kept, including handing over Annabel.

It was a bad position to be in, no matter how you looked at it. But ultimately Harvey had decided there was only one way to go. He had to take the chance that Annabel would be returned if he did what the Alpha asked. At least that gave her a shot at surviving the night. If the KP crew went after the guttata, Harvey had no doubt their leader would carry out his threat to eliminate Annabel.

Harvey was certain of this for a very good reason. Several years before, he had been in a situation similar to this one. That time Harvey had gone after his enemy . . . and had lost one of Killer Pizza's most valuable MCOs as a result of his gamble.

That MCO had been Harvey's brother.

It was a decision that would haunt Harvey for the rest of his life. No way was he going to gamble this time around. So all he could do now was wait. And hope, come morning, that Annabel would walk through Killer Pizza's front door, safe and sound.

■ ■ ■

The jostling finally stopped. Annabel had not managed to loosen the rope binding her wrists, not even the slightest bit, so she lay still and listened. The back door of the vehicle suddenly swung open. Annabel felt someone cut the ropes that bound her ankles. The hand that took her by the arm and guided her slowly out of the vehicle was surprisingly gentle. Annabel expected much rougher treatment, especially after getting smacked in the head and being abducted from her home.

"Hello."

Annabel was startled to hear the sudden greeting. The hand holding Annabel's arm indicated for her to stop. "Sorry about the inconvenience, young lady," the voice continued. "You seem like a nice enough person. Of course, you have no one to blame but yourself for this predicament. You shouldn't have gotten involved with such bad company."

Annabel kept her face impassive. A mask.

"We'll get to know each other better soon enough. Until then, my associates will take you to a nice, comfortable room. That's the least you deserve after such a trying journey."

As the hand holding Annabel got her moving again, Annabel was seized with a sudden urge to lash out at her captor. This could be it, after all. Her only chance of escape. But when a second person grabbed her other arm, that squelched any thought of a fight for freedom. Annabel knew she couldn't take on two people while blindfolded, gagged, and with her hands tied behind her back. So she allowed herself to be led wherever it was she was going, concentrating instead on sensory signposts, anything that might indicate where she had been taken. Sounds. Smells. Anything.

But Annabel was having trouble focusing. She wished she hadn't heard that disembodied voice. In spite of the pleasant words, there was a quality to it that creeped her out. The flat, unemotional tone made Annabel think of blackened, leafless trees.

As Annabel was led up a stairway, tentacles of fear began to work their way through her body, like some kind of virus. She'd been able to fight that sensation when she was in the car. But no longer. It was the voice that had done it.

Now all Annabel could think was: Did anyone know where she was? Was anyone coming to her aid? She certainly hoped so. After her sightless meeting with her captor (he was the Alpha, Annabel was certain), she knew she was in trouble.

Big-time.

6

Strobe's powerful legs were a blur as they propelled Toby's bike rapidly down the hot, deserted suburban street. Sitting on a seat that had been fashioned over the rear wheel fender, Toby held on tight.

The two were an odd sight. Beside the fact that the bike was too small for them, Toby was wearing not one but *two* overstuffed backpacks, and Strobe had the strange-looking aluminum tube strapped across his back.

"What is this thing, anyway?" Toby asked, referring to the tube.

"A CSG," Strobe said as he negotiated a sharp turn.

"Which means?"

"Creature stun gun. Packs an amazing wallop."

"How do you know? Ever use it?"

"No."

"Bring any instructions?"

"No. But how hard can it be? We'll figure it out."

"That thing looks pretty unwieldy, man."

"Just think how difficult it was to get it out of KP without anyone noticing. Trust me, we'll be happy we have it. From what I read, hitting a bull's-eye in the dark would be easier than nailing the Alpha's DDI."

"Wow. I'm impressed you know about the depressor dens inferiorus, Strobe."

"What can I say? I've been reading my text. You may applaud me."

Protected by impenetrable, fossilized bone, the depressor dens inferioris was a small depression at the back of an Alpha's neck. The thing that had caught Strobe's eye as he read about the DDI: just before an Alpha attacked its prey, the protective plate over the DDI opened for a split second, exposing the vulnerable area. Considering that the Alpha's heart was *never* vulnerable—it was completely encased by a crucible of the same steel-like bone that covered the DDI—this made the DDI the lone "Achilles heel" of an Alpha Male guttata. Nail the exposed depressor dens inferiorus, so long, Alpha. But as Strobe pointed out, that was an almost impossible task.

Hence, the CSG.

"Where are we going, by the way?" Toby asked as he and Strobe blasted down a steep hill, the rush of wind blowing their sweat-wet hair back from their faces.

"To the Brentwood police station."

"Why?"

"Before we do battle with Alpha Man, we have to find out who he is, right?"

"I believe that's a given."

"Okay, so we're gonna use Gome to point the way."

"How so?"

"You and I are about to do some good old-fashioned police work." Strobe took a left at the bottom of the hill and pedaled down the middle of the asphalt street as heat lightning flashed in the distance. Toby wasn't sure what Strobe had in mind, but it already made him nervous.

■ ■ ■

"Well? What do you think?"

Toby and Strobe had found a hiding place for the bike and their gear in a wooded area about a block away from the police station. Pacing back and forth in the woods, Toby had a concerned frown on his face.

"I don't know. This sounds like a pretty far-out plan to me."

"You have a better idea?"

"No. But maybe you should have the seizure. I'll go find Gome's office."

"You want to find Gome's office? Fine. I'll do the seizure."

Toby tried to imagine himself scurrying around the police station in an attempt to find Gome's office while Strobe pretended to have a seizure in the lobby. He wasn't sure if he could handle that. "Okay, let's go back to your original plan. I'll have the seizure."

"Sure?"

"Yeah, I'm sure."

"Let's get to it, then. We don't have all the time in the world here."

Now Toby tried to picture himself pretending to have a seizure in the lobby of the Brentwood Hills borough building. It was just acting, right?

Acting?! Toby had never set foot near a stage his entire life. What did *he* know about acting? Nothing. Absolutely nothing. Toby gulped nervously, then followed Strobe out of the woods.

■ ■ ■

"Unnnnnggggghhhhhh!!!"

Toby rolled up his eyes and fell heavily to the floor

at the base of the steps that led up to the lobby of the borough building. He cracked his head when he went down and almost blacked out from the blow. His eyes literally glazed over, the result of skull meeting floor.

Okay, that really hurt! But use *it! Use the pain!*

The receptionist who greeted visitors to the borough building immediately left her desk, ran down the stairs, and knelt by Toby's side. Summoned by the receptionist's calls for help, two police officers pushed through the door that led to the police-station half of the building and began tending to Toby.

Time for Strobe to make his move.

He had been waiting outside the front entrance to the building. Toby had used the back parking lot entrance. Now Strobe entered the building and moved quickly across the lobby. He checked to make sure no one was watching him, then opened the door marked POLICE and eased it shut behind him.

Strobe found himself facing a short hallway. After a few long strides, he stopped and peered cautiously into a large room at the end of the hall. There were three desks for police assistants. Each assistant was positioned near a police officer's door.

Fortunately, the place had almost emptied out as a result of Toby's seizure pantomime. There was only one assistant, her back to Strobe, and one officer's silhouette behind the glazed glass of his office window. It didn't take long for Strobe to spot the office door with THOMAS GOME painted on it.

Keeping close to the wall, Strobe edged his way toward Gome's office. He was now shielded from the lone assistant by a partition that surrounded three quarters of her desk. Just as Strobe slipped into Gome's office, a shrill, distant siren blasted the air outside.

Paramedics.

The countdown had begun. Strobe definitely didn't want Toby to have to deal with them. That would complicate things. Pulling a digital camera out of his pocket, Strobe started snapping away at the diplomas and pictures Gome had on his walls. As he moved to Gome's desk . . .

"What's going on out there, Vicki?"

Strobe dove under the desk when he heard the officer talking to his assistant just outside Gome's closed door.

"I don't know."

"You're really *on* it, aren't you?"

The two laughed. There was more conversation between the two, but it was muted. Strobe couldn't hear them. He wiped a bead of sweat away from his temple with the back of his hand. This wasn't good. The paramedics would arrive before he knew it and he was totally trapped in Gome's office!

Strobe took a few more pictures of Gome's desk, all the while hearing the low murmur of talk between the policeman and his assistant, the blurry silhouette of the officer visible through the pebbled glass of the window.

By now the sirens were just down the road. Definitely time to go. Strobe took one last picture, pocketed his camera, and stared at the door. The two were still out there. Strobe looked at the window. It was the only way out.

■ ■ ■

"Anybody comin'?"

Strobe glanced over his shoulder at the borough building. "Not yet." He and Toby were hustling it across the parking lot toward the woods where they had stashed the bicycle. It had been a very close call, with Strobe rescuing Toby just before the paramedics arrived, ad-libbing to the perplexed crowd that his brother had a strange condition that produced seizures from time to time when he went from the humid heat of the outdoors to the air-conditioned chill of the indoors. There was no known cure for the mysterious ailment, other than to stay indoors—or outdoors—all summer long!

"You were really somethin', Tobe," Strobe said as they double-timed it across a couple of tennis courts. The woods were just on the other side of the courts. "I almost called the paramedics, you were so convincing."

"Let's just hope this was worth it."

When Strobe and Toby got to the shelter of the woods, they immediately started going through the pictures on Strobe's camera. The images included: Gome getting some kind of award . . . Gome with the Brentwood Hills Board of Directors . . . Gome at some kind of "breaking-ground" ceremony . . . Gome standing on a pier by a lake, proudly holding up a large trout.

"Know any of the people in these pictures?" Strobe asked.

"No."

"How 'bout this one?" Strobe went back to the image of Gome with the Board of Directors. "Maybe Alpha Man is one of these dudes. Know any of them?"

"No. Besides, why would Gome want to hang a picture of him with one of his gargoyle pals in his office?"

"Why wouldn't he? Nobody around here even knows guttata exist."

Strobe had a point there.

"What do we do now?" Toby asked, disappointed in the outcome of their siege on the Brentwood Hills police station.

"Get a move on."

Strobe could see a couple of paramedics outside the borough building, scanning the area. After pulling on their backpacks, the two swung onto the bicycle—this time with Toby steering—and took off through the woods. Emerging into an open field on the other side of the woods, Toby bounced down a short hill, over a curb, and pedaled past the row of houses that lined one side of the street.

"Let's go back to your place," Strobe said. "I'm not willing to give up on these pictures. I want to put them on your computer. Blow 'em up. We might be able to find some kind of clue in the details."

"Like that movie, right? The one where the guy, the fashion photographer, takes some pictures of that girl . . ."

"Never saw it. Just . . . get us to your place, okay?"

At the end of the street, Toby spotted one of several entrances to the vast acreage of North Park. He steered his bike into the park and onto one of the walking trails. As the bike shot past a large playground, something suddenly caught Strobe's eye.

"*Stop!*" Strobe yelled.

Strobe's command caused Toby to lose control of the precariously overloaded bike. His teeth chattered as the bike swerved from the walking trail and bounced over the exposed roots of a large maple tree. It was like riding over railroad ties.

If only that trash can hadn't been in the way.

Toby was on his back, staring up at the sky, before he knew what hit him. Looking around, he saw Strobe running toward the playground. "Strobe! What the . . . ?"

But Strobe was already out of earshot. When Toby caught up to him he was standing near a plaque at the edge of the playground. The plaque read: FOR THE ENJOYMENT OF THE FUTURE MOTHERS AND FATHERS AND LEADERS OF THE NORTH PARK AREA COMMUNITIES. Looking through the pictures on his camera, Strobe nodded when he found the picture of the breaking-ground ceremony.

"Check it out," he said, handing the camera to Toby. Sure enough, the ceremony depicted in the picture—before the playground had been built—had taken place at the very spot where Strobe and Toby now stood.

"So?" Toby asked.

"So? You know what this is, Tobe? Serendipity. I think we were meant to ride past this playground at this particular moment in time. Ten to one the guy in that picture is Alpha Man."

Toby studied the picture. Gome stood next to a man who was taking the first shovel of dirt out of the ground where the future playground would be built. He was a very tall, youngish-looking man with silver hair.

"You think this is our man because of serendipity? What's that mean, anyway?"

"You know, when something happens . . . something good, usually, I think . . . by chance."

"I seem to remember you telling Annabel not to get all mystical on us when she said she was *meant* to come to Killer Pizza."

"Yeah, well . . . this is different."

"How so?"

"This is more than just a feeling. I mean, look at the guy. That silver hair?"

"Plenty of people have prematurely gray hair."

"That's not prematurely gray. It looks like alien hair. Think about this. A monster donating money for a kid's playground? C'mon. It's just too perfect!"

7

Annabel heard someone come into the room. Still
bound and gagged, she was sitting in a large, cushioned
chair. At least she'd been comfortable for the past hour
while she waited to discover what her captors had in
store for her.

Annabel jumped when she felt hands at the back of
her head, untying her gag. Now the blindfold came
off. Annabel sat very still, staring straight ahead. The
person who had untied her gag walked slowly into
view, crossed the room, and sat in a chair opposite
Annabel.

"Good evening," a man with silver hair said.

Like his voice, the man's appearance was chilling. He
was impeccably dressed. A Rolex watch glinted on his
wrist. A gold earring reflected the light from a nearby
lamp. But in spite of all the window dressing, there was

something hollow about him. Annabel felt like she was looking at a living dead man.

"You're Takashi Oshiro's daughter."

Annabel's stomach turned. This man knew her *father*?

The silver-haired man gave Annabel a look that was strangely sympathetic. "Don't worry. Your father is not one of us. I know him socially. That's all."

That's actually the thought that had gripped Annabel—that her father might be a guttata!

"No, your father is much too successful to be a candidate for my pack. You see, I only take in people who need me. Whom I can help. I run a very charitable organization, when you come right down to it. I find people who have 'holes' in their lives, as I like to say, and give them everything they've ever dreamed of."

Annabel wanted to respond that the only thing these people had to give in return were their human souls, but she held her tongue.

The man stood and walked to a bar in the corner of the room. "Anyway, I'm sure that you're anxious to know why you're here."

"Yes, I am. I'm going to be late for work if you keep me any longer. I have the evening shift at Killer Pizza."

The words surprised Annabel when she said them. She hadn't worked out any kind of plan on how to deal with Alpha Man.

"Don't play dumb with me, Miss Oshiro. I know you don't work in Killer Pizza's kitchen. One of my associates observed you at the Child house the night Child made his unfortunate return. It's clear you're involved with a group of people who seem intent on my destruction."

"I don't know what you're talking about. I just make specialty pizzas."

The man stared at Annabel. He nodded slowly, then returned to his chair and sat down. "I'm going to tell you a little story. I think you'll find it informative."

The silver-haired man explained about the ultimatum he had given Annabel's people. The ultimatum seemed to have worked. No one had followed any of his pack to the Gathering, so far as he could tell. Which meant that no one was coming to Annabel's aid.

Annabel tried not to show how devastated she was, hearing that.

"But I still have a problem here," the man continued. "I have no idea who your boss is. No idea what kind of organization he's running. Simply that his headquarters seem to be in the unfortunately named Killer Pizza building on Industrial Avenue. All this makes me very uneasy."

The man crossed his legs and smoothed out a wrinkle in his perfectly tailored trousers.

"Which is where you come in. I am prepared to offer you a way out of this very nasty situation that has befallen you. All you have to do is tell me who you work for. His name. The extent of his organization. Do that, and you will be able to make it in time for your evening shift at the pizza shop."

The man stared at Annabel with an amused, reptilian-like expression on his face. The only sound in the room was of music, coming from a lower floor.

"On the other hand, if you don't tell me what I need to know about my unknown adversary? And this is the lovely part." The man paused before delivering the punch line. "I will welcome you into my pack."

Annabel had the strange sensation of falling, even as she sat still in her chair. Vertigo.

"Oh, come now, Miss Oshiro. Don't look so alarmed. This is actually an *opportunity* I'm presenting to you. Granted, there is that little bit of unpleasantness when you make the transition. But afterward . . . you can't even imagine how wonderful it is. Ask any of the people downstairs. After getting a taste of my world, you will do anything to protect it. *Anything.* Including giving me whatever information I need about the people you work with."

Annabel couldn't believe what she was hearing. She was struggling to hold herself together, not fall completely apart.

The man suddenly stood and walked toward Annabel. She struggled against her ropes. She didn't want this guy anywhere near her. "I'm sorry to have to run," she heard him say as he circled around her, put the gag back across her mouth, and tied it. "But the time for my appearance at the Gathering is at hand." Annabel flinched when the man bent down close to her. "You understand, I'm sure."

The man stopped before exiting and looked back at Annabel. When he smiled, Annabel thought she saw a couple of unnervingly sharp incisor teeth. Had they been like that before?

"So this is good, yes?" the man said. "You have a little time to think things over. The choice is yours. Return to your people. Or join my side. Either way, I get what I want."

Annabel now noticed that a stream of saliva had

started to run down one side of the man's chin. What a repulsive sight! The man took out a handkerchief and calmly wiped his chin clean. Then he gave Annabel a courtly nod and closed the door quietly behind him as he left the room.

Annabel sat stock-still in her chair. She still felt as though she were falling. But now she knew where she was falling *to*.

That would be right into the middle of hell.

8

The silver-haired man's name was Farrior.

That's what Strobe was able to discover after getting a Brentwood Hills councilman on the phone and explaining that he was doing an article for the fall edition of his high school newspaper on newsworthy people who had done "good works" for the local communities. After thanking the councilman for his time and suggestions, Strobe called directory assistance to get Farrior's phone number and address.

"He lives in Shadyside," Strobe announced, referring to an exclusive, upper-class area located about twenty miles from Hidden Hills. He bounced off of Toby's bed and pocketed his cell phone. "Let's go."

"Hold on a second, Strobe. We need to call Harvey now, right?"

"No way. You better believe Harvey's phone is

bugged. We can't get in touch with him until we have Annabel."

"But Shadyside . . . that's like, miles and miles from here. I'm not biking over there."

"Obviously."

"So . . . a bus?"

"Nightmare. Figuring out the schedule? Transfers? Been there, done that. It'd take us forever, and we don't have a lot of time to work with here. What about that car in the garage?"

"Don't even—"

"I know how to drive, Tobe."

"We're not taking my mom's car. End of story."

"Annabel's *life* is in danger. Who cares if we break a law or two?"

Strobe was right about that. If ever there was a time to toss aside concerns about breaking a law or two, this would be it.

"I'm pretty sure I heard Mom say there's something wrong with the engine," Toby suddenly remembered. "The check engine light, or something like that, keeps going on."

"I'm handy with a car. I'll deal with whatever comes up."

Toby thought about the possible consequences of taking his mother's car. What if it died on them? What if they did something to it that Harvey and his crew couldn't take care of? How would he ever be able to explain that to his parents?

The high-pitched whine of a sander could be heard downstairs, where the KP workers were smoothing out the grooves left in the living room floor by Child's talons. Toby couldn't help but smile and shake his head at the ridiculous scenario.

"What?" Strobe asked.

"Nothin'. Just thinkin' about how deep I'm in already. Why not add car theft to my list of sins?"

"Don't worry. I'll treat your mom's car as though it were my own."

"That's *exactly* what I'm worried about."

■ ■ ■

A half hour later, Strobe was turning Toby's mother's Subaru onto Old Hickory Lane in Shadyside.

Toby couldn't believe they were already here. Things were happening too fast for him. He felt like he needed more time to prepare, to gear up for this rescue operation. But there was no more time. The time was *now*. Right here, in this neighborhood, *on this street*, was where the Gathering was being held!

Strobe pulled to the curb and stopped in front of one of the palatial homes that were set back on lush, expansive lawns. A turn in the road obscured their view of the rest of the street. "Farrior's place has to be right around the corner. Ready?"

Toby nodded, even though he wasn't. He opened the door and got out of the car. He and Strobe were silent as they walked toward Farrior's house. The two had already talked about various game plans on their way to Shady-side, had decided they needed to stake out Farrior's house first, then wait until dark to make their move. Coming around the bend in the street, Toby was suddenly aware of how dry his mouth was. He couldn't spit to save his life.

Heart pounding. Dry mouth. Was this fun, or what?!

"That's it," Strobe suddenly said, pulling Toby behind a nearby hedge. "The one straight ahead. That's Farrior's."

The two stared from behind their leafy barrier at Farrior's impressive, castle-like stone mansion, located at the end of a cul-de-sac. Even on a street lined with gorgeous, one-of-a-kind residences, the place was immense, regal, by comparison.

But there was something wrong with it.

At least from Strobe's and Toby's points of view. There

was no sign of activity in the house or anywhere on the large grounds. No cars. No people. No music or lively chatter. *Nothing.*

"Maybe they're in the basement or something," Toby said. "I mean, who knows what goes on during this new moon rave?"

"Harvey said there could be hundreds of people in this pack. What'd they do, turn guttata and *fly* in? In broad daylight?"

"Actually, Strobe, the pack isn't able to turn guttata a few days before or after a Gathering. It's a hormonal thing. Alphas aren't affected by it. I guess you didn't read that part in the text. Besides, only Alphas are able to fly, right?"

Toby instantly shut up when Strobe turned a laser-like glare at him. Strobe held his intimidating gaze for a few moments, then resumed looking at the house with the gone-for-the-weekend look.

"Can't believe this," Strobe said in disgust. "Either the party's somewhere else, or Farrior isn't our guy. We're busted, either way. Back to square one."

Toby could feel the negative vibes oozing from Strobe. That was to be expected. This was a bummer, after all. But what happened next was totally unexpected. Just like *that*, without warning—Strobe snapped.

Toby was startled when Strobe started to punch and yank at their leafy hiding place! Leaves flew every-where! Branches were ripped from the hedge and tossed into the air!

"Strobe! Calm down! We could get arrested for at-tacking a hedge around here!"

Toby had to separate Strobe from the perfectly trimmed bush. He managed to pull him back to the sidewalk before Strobe—looking like he wanted to go at the hedge again—pushed him away.

"Wait a second!" Toby commanded. "Just hold on. I have an idea."

Strobe still looked like he was breathing fire. Toby knew he had to talk fast.

"Harvey gave me and Annabel a quick course in bur-glary. Remember? I'll get in there and see what I can find out. Like you said, maybe they're having the party somewhere else."

At least Toby's suggestion got rid of the wild look in Strobe's eyes. But Strobe didn't look very impressed with the idea. "Look at that place," he said. "It's gotta have the most sophisticated alarm system on the planet. No way you'll be able to crack it."

Okay, maybe Strobe had a point there. Toby's mind whirled as he tried to latch on to something else that might rescue them from their disappointing dead end. Something. *Anything.*

"Let me see the camera."

"What for? We've already gone through—"

"Hand it over!"

The force of Toby's exclamation surprised Strobe. He meekly reached into his pocket and handed the camera to Toby. Clicking through the pictures, Toby didn't linger over any of them. He knew what he was looking for. He stopped when he got to the picture of Gome holding up his trophy trout. Toby handed the camera to Strobe. "That might be Echo Lake."

"So?"

"This friend of mine? He used to live on my street. But then his dad got a better job, or a promotion or something, and they moved to a better part of Hidden Hills."

"And you've felt bad ever since, 'cause this guy eventually moved on and got a whole new group of friends."

"Actually, that's true. But the point is, my former friend's dad bought a place at Echo Lake. I went up there a couple of times. It's where a lot of rich people have their second homes. Maybe Farrior has a place up there. It could be *his* place where this picture of Gome was taken. Makes sense, don't you think? Them having their monthly deal up there? An out-of-the-way place, instead of right here in the middle of Shadyside?"

Strobe chewed on this new information for a moment, then nodded thoughtfully. "You might be on to something, Tobe."

Toby smiled. He just might have cracked the Gathering location mystery!

"How far is it to this Echo Lake?"

"About an hour and a half."

"I'll get us there in an hour."

9

The sign up ahead read PLEASANT HILLS. **In spite of the** tense atmosphere in the car, Toby couldn't help but perk up when he saw the sign.

"Hey, that's where they have a farmer's market, last Friday of each month. I read about it in the paper. It's supposed to be really great. They have all this fantastic stuff you can't buy in the local groceries. Vegetables. Cheeses." Toby was getting increasingly excited as he thought about the market. "I could really use some mascarpone cheese for a chicken marsala dish I want to try. Some cipollini onions would be nice, too."

Strobe slowly turned his head and gave Toby an incredulous look. "You're not suggesting we stop at an outdoor market on our way to rescue Annabel, are you, Tobe?"

Toby felt his cheeks get red. "No . . . of course not. Just pointing it out, is all."

"Uh-huh."

Toby turned away from Strobe and looked out the window as Strobe shot up a ramp and onto a bridge. Behind them, the city. Ahead, on the horizon, a mountain range. Echo Lake.

Don't know where else I'm gonna get that mascarpone, though, Toby thought as they crossed the bridge and headed into open country. Then he noted the setting sun on the horizon. By the time they arrived in Echo Lake, darkness would have fallen. The Gathering would have begun. *If* they were going to the right place.

Discarding images of cheeses and onions, Toby focused on what he hoped they would find up at Echo Lake. He knew he would have to use everything he had learned over the past month, and then some, to be of any help in this rescue operation. But first Toby had to stifle a dreadful thought that had been nagging at him.

Wherever Annabel was, what if she'd already been harmed by her captors?

Toby glanced over at Strobe. Staring out the windshield at the distant hills, Strobe's expression was blank. Unreadable. But Toby had a feeling that his KP partner was worried about the same thing.

. . .

The long-haired, sleepy-eyed clerk behind the counter of the only market in Echo Lake looked at the picture of Farrior on Strobe's camera with a perplexed frown.

"Oh, yeah. Sure, I recognize *him*," the clerk said. "Didn't know his name was Farrior. I thought it was Farrington. Farwell. Somethin' like that."

Strobe and Toby simultaneously issued silent prayers of thanks. They hadn't hit a dead end, after all. Earlier, Toby had called directory assistance on his cell phone to get Farrior's address in Echo Lake but was told no one by that name was listed in the mountain community. Toby and Strobe had decided to press on, anyway, take their chances Farrior had an unlisted number. What else could they do? They had no other leads. It was Desperation Time.

"Everyone 'round here calls that guy Log Cabin," the clerk said as he sliced open a carton of cigarettes. "He's kind of the standoffish type, you know? But then, there are a lot of those types up here. Not the ones who live here year-round, of course."

"You know where Farrior lives?" Strobe asked. He was anxious to get going. It was already dark outside.

"Yeah . . . Let's see . . . got an address here somewhere. We make deliveries over there from time to time. Actually, just did a few days ago. They seem to have a big party over there about once a month, now I think about it."

Toby and Strobe exchanged excited glances. Once-a-month parties? Farrior *had* to be their guy! The clerk found the address, wrote it down, and handed it to Strobe.

"Thanks, man," Strobe said as he headed for the door.

"Hey . . . Be careful over there."

That got Strobe's and Toby's attention.

"Why?" Toby asked.

"Word is those parties can be kinda wild." The clerk gave Toby and Strobe a you-know-what-I-mean kind of wink.

"Rrrrrright," Strobe replied. "Thanks for the tip."

"That you *won't* get from the dude. Not much of one, anyway. If you were making a delivery, that is. Can you believe it? He's only one of the richest guys around. But then, that's what they say about rich people, right? They're rich *because* they're so stingy. This one time? I took about three hundred dollars' worth of groceries to this guy down the road. He's the owner of, like, some kind of *Internet* thing, I don't really get how they make so much money, it's not like they're making anything solid . . . But, anyway, I take this stuff down to him . . ."

Strobe and Toby waved and slipped out the door as the clerk continued his story about the miserly rich. They didn't want to be rude or anything, but they had some business to tend to.

■ ■ ■

The Subaru finally gave out on the way to Farrior's house. No sputtering, no lurching, no warning, just . . . done. Strobe pulled over to the shoulder of the dark two-lane road and coasted to a stop.

"Good Sub," Strobe said. "She got us here, anyway."

"We have time to fix it?" Toby asked.

"No way. We gotta move, man."

"But how are we gonna get back?"

"We'll cross that bridge when we have to. First we get Annabel away from any danger. Then we'll call Harvey. C'mon, let's motor."

Strobe and Toby gathered up their gear and jogged off down the road. They had gone about a mile when they arrived at the driveway to Farrior's Echo Lake retreat. Strobe pulled Toby into the woods after confirming that the address on a stone mailbox next to the driveway was the one they were looking for.

"Probably have all kinds of security cameras around here," Strobe said as he pulled his NVGs out of his backpack. "We're not about to walk right down the driveway, that's for sure." Putting on his goggles, Strobe looked off through the trees. Farrior's house had not been visible from the road. But from this vantage point, the glitter of lights could be seen in the distance.

"Let's go," Strobe said. He started off toward the house. Toby fell in behind him. When they got closer to the glittering lights they were able to hear music, drifting through the pines. *Disco* music. Weird. The thumping beat got louder and louder as Strobe and Toby made their way through the dark forest. Their trek was interrupted by an eight-foot-tall, barred security fence. There, on the other side of the fence, was Farrior's "log cabin."

A massive, three-story, modern version of a log cabin, that is. Lights blazed in the house. Dozens of vehicles were parked on the side of a long circular driveway that curved around in front of the entrance to Farrior's getaway home. A mass of people was visible through the windows on the first floor, movin' and groovin' to the music.

The Gathering.

Strobe and Toby hid behind the trunk of a large

pine, dug into their backpacks, and pulled out their infrared binoculars. "How on earth are we gonna get in there?" Toby asked after studying the fortress-like complex that stretched out in front of him. "There must be more than a hundred people at this shindig!"

Strobe was eying the lone lit window on the third floor through his binoculars. "I think maybe just I go in. You stay here, be lookout."

"What are you talking about?" Toby asked, surprised at Strobe's suggestion.

"This is the best way."

"How do you figure?"

"I need someone to be my eyes out here. Get your headset on."

Toby could tell there was no point in arguing with Strobe. The guy's mind was obviously made up. As Toby rummaged in his pack for his headset, Strobe said, "Keep in touch." Then he was off.

Toby watched Strobe disappear into the dark night. Actually, it was *beyond* dark. The dense blanket of pine branches overhead, coupled with the new moon—when no moon is visible—tipped the visual scales from dark to pitch-black.

All Toby could do now was wait for word from

Strobe. And watch for any suspicious activity around the house.

■ ■ ■

"Ommmmph!"

Strobe hit the ground and instantly rolled to try to break some of the impact. The roll might have helped a bit more if Strobe hadn't had the bazooka-like CSG strapped across his back. He had figured out how to use the thing on the way up to Echo Lake—and had elected to take the bulky weapon over the fence with him instead of his crossbow. Which meant he resembled a severely flat tire as he thumped and wobbled across the lawn, finally coming to a halt on the dew-covered grass.

The wind having been knocked out of him, Strobe lay still for a moment, then rolled over, pushed himself to his feet, and ran to the side of the house, which was cloaked in shadow.

"You okay?" Toby asked over the headset.

"Yeah," Strobe replied. "I'm gonna try the back way."

Hugging the house, Strobe moved away from the front rooms, where the party was being held. It sounded as though the celebration was reaching a fever pitch. It sounded *wild* in there. No way did Strobe want to deal with those people if he could possibly help it.

When Strobe turned the corner at the rear of the house he heard voices in the darkness ahead. Two men, standing on a pier at the bottom of a sloping lawn. Strobe instantly shrank back into the shadows, stood stock-still, and waited to see if he had been noticed.

He hadn't. Strobe shifted his gaze from the men to a nearby set of French doors that were opened onto the patio. He was tempted. Should he make a run for the doors or find another way to get into the house?

A woman suddenly appeared at the open French doors. It was the blue-eyed woman. Strobe didn't like the look of her. Dangerous. Definitely dangerous. The woman stood silently for a moment, staring out into the night, then walked down the lawn to join the two men on the pier.

The woman's appearance at the back door seemed to answer Strobe's question. Too risky going in the back way.

But how else to get in? No telling how many people were in the house or where they would be at any given moment. Getting inside was looking to be a very tricky deal. Strobe decided to go back the way he had come.

"Strobe, what's wrong?" Toby asked from his vantage point beyond the fence when he saw him.

"People back there. I need another way in." Strobe stopped when he was directly under the lit third-story window and looked up. He felt one of the logs that made up the exterior of the house. He put his foot up on another log, testing it. Then he rubbed his hands together and gave himself a nod.

He had found his other way in.

■ ■ ■

"Strobe? Are you *crazy*?" Toby watched through his binoculars as Strobe began his climb up the side of the house.

"I have a feeling Annabel's up in that top room," Strobe replied. "If not, I'll work my way through the house from there."

"If you fall you won't be any help to Annabel. Or me. You could break your neck goin' up that way!"

"I don't intend to fall. I did a little sheer rock climbing when I lived in Colorado. But, hey, thanks for the vote of confidence."

Toby was already getting a jolt of vertigo just from watching Strobe. His eyes flitted from his friend to the dancing silhouettes behind the windows at the front of the house to the dark areas around the large grounds.

Strobe made steady, impressive progress up the

sheer wall of the house. He was about halfway to his destination when the three people from the backyard walked into view.

"Strobe!" Toby hissed over his headset.

Strobe instantly froze. Toby watched helplessly as the woman and two men walked slowly along the side yard. One of the men was Gome, his bald head shining in the night. Talking intently, the threesome were soon directly beneath Strobe. All they had to do was look up and they'd see him!

Strobe was somewhat sheltered by a shadow cast by the large stone fireplace chimney that stretched from the first floor to the third. But Toby was alarmed to see that the metallic barrel of the CSG was catching some light from a nearby second-story window and glinting in the darkness.

"Please . . . keep going," Toby prayed. As though they had heard Toby's whispered plea, the three suddenly stopped!

Toby went rigid with fear. He stared breathlessly at the three as they stood in the shadow of the house, then saw the flare of a lighter glow in the darkness. Gome was lighting the woman's cigarette.

It wasn't until they had resumed their walk toward

the front yard, had gone up the front steps to the large wraparound porch and disappeared inside the house that Toby allowed himself a sigh of relief.

"That was close, man."

"Next stop, third floor," Strobe replied.

■ ■ ■

When he got there, his hands grasping the lower sill of the window, his feet lodged on the top of a log below, Strobe peeked cautiously into the room. He felt his heart leap when he saw Annabel, sitting in a chair across the room. But his elation was quickly cut by anger. No, it was more than anger. Seeing Annabel bound and gagged filled Strobe with an intense rage, a boiling, over-the-top emotion he'd never felt before. He knew he had to contain that feeling, however. He couldn't let emotion get in the way of what needed to be done.

"Strobe! What's goin' on?" Toby's voice was muted, as though it was having a difficult time traveling the distance between Strobe and him.

"She's here," Strobe responded. He delicately maneuvered over and up until he was in a position to be able to grasp the frame of the lower part of the window. It took a few tries, but Strobe was finally able to open the window.

Alerted by the sound, Annabel stared at Strobe as he

eased himself into the room. Her expression wasn't what Strobe was expecting, however. Instead of being happy to see him, Annabel looked concerned. Panicked, even.

"Greetings, young man."

Strobe whirled to see Farrior standing by the bar in the corner, casually mixing a drink. The intense vibes that emanated from him filled the room, held Strobe motionless. Strobe knew he was in the presence of someone—some*thing*—extraordinary, that's for sure.

"I don't get involved in that ruckus downstairs," Farrior said pleasantly. "Once I'm done giving them what they need, it's their party, their time to let loose. I don't mind being the designated driver, so to speak. I have to look out for my people, after all."

Strobe was dismayed at how he was reacting to Alpha Man. His hands were shaking. His knees felt weak. He willed himself to focus on one thing: getting Annabel out of this monster pit. That's what he was here for.

Strobe stepped toward her. Farrior mimicked his movement with a smile. "In other words," Farrior said, picking up where he had left off, "I don't wish for you to interrupt my little get-together. And you won't. I'll see to that. When my people are sleeping off their fun later on, you'll be sleeping with the fishes. Sorry, an over-used expression, I know. But it's one I happen to like."

Farrior's casual, engaging manner suddenly disappeared. It was as though a switch inside the man had been abruptly flicked off.

Blood ran cold.

Strobe suddenly knew what that expression truly meant. He felt like his blood was no longer warming his body. The man facing him had absolutely chilled him to the bone.

"Your commander in chief, whoever he may be, should know better than to send a *kid* to do his dirty work," Farrior said, the disgust obvious in his voice. "I'll take no pleasure in dispatching you to the hereafter. But I do promise I'll make it quick."

Strobe knew he had one shot at saving Annabel. And himself. Ready or not, he was about to take it.

10

KA-BOOOOOOM!!!

Toby jerked in surprise when he heard the explosive sound erupt from the third-story window.

"Strobe! What happened?"

Strobe didn't respond. Toby instantly felt an explosion of emotions—fear-concern-panic-"OH-MY-GOD-WHAT-TO-DO?!!"—slam through his veins.

"Strobe! Answer me! What's goin' on?!"

No reply.

The blast from the CSG had been so loud it had cut through the music downstairs and brought the party to a screeching halt. Several people bounded onto the porch and scanned the grounds. It was clear they weren't sure where the explosion had come from.

KA-BOOOOOM!!!

Another blast from the third-story window. Panicked yells from inside. The people on the porch turned and ran back into the house.

Toby grabbed his backpack and ran to the fence. He had to get in there! Try to help somehow!

"Toby!" Strobe's voice suddenly crackled over the headset.

"Strobe! Where are you?"

"Comin' out! Meet me at the front gate. Get ready for action!"

Toby was frozen for a moment, then grabbed his crossbow from his pack and quickly assembled it. He slapped on his bicep plate—the extra arrow cartridge already attached—grabbed Strobe's backpack from the ground, and ran in the direction of the front gate.

Even though he had the benefit of his NVGs, Toby could barely see his way through the dark maze of pines. He banged his arm painfully against a tree trunk, stumbled over a tree root, barely managed to stay upright, then continued his blind rush through the woods.

KA-BOOOOM!!!

A third blast from the house, echoing among the pine trees!

"You okay, Strobe?" Toby yelled into his headset. "I'm on my way!"

Finally, there it was. Toby could see the front gate off to his left. He broke from the forest and blazed down the driveway, passing several cars that had been parked outside the gate.

There! There they were! Toby felt a wave of relief when he saw Strobe and Annabel on the other side of the fence, sprinting across the front yard.

But just behind them were three people. Gome. The blue-eyed woman. And the other man from the backyard. Toby skidded to a stop just as Strobe and Annabel hit the fence at a run and started to climb. He tossed Strobe's backpack to the ground and aimed his crossbow through the bars of the fence. Focusing on the lead man—Gome—he pulled the trigger.

Gome cried out as he grabbed his side and fell to the grass. At the top of the fence, Annabel leaped and grabbed hold of a nearby pine branch. Strobe was right behind her.

Toby fired again, this time spinning the other man around when his arrow penetrated the man's shoulder. Before he was able to get off another shot, the blue-eyed woman slammed into the fence and grabbed for him.

Startled at the woman's ferocity, Toby accidentally fired his crossbow—the arrow thudding harmlessly into the ground—as he stumbled away from the fence. Even though Toby knew the woman couldn't turn guttata at this time of month, he had no doubt she could rip him to shreds just the same. She had that look about her: a blisteringly feral, primitive spark in those ruthless blue eyes of hers.

Surprisingly, the woman didn't make a move to get over the fence to attack Toby. She didn't back off when Toby raised the crossbow to his shoulder, either. Instead, she *smiled*. A mirthless, hair-raising smile that gave Toby the chills.

"You have no idea what you're dealing with here, little man." Toby couldn't take his eyes off the woman. It was as though she had hypnotized him or something.

SMASH!!!

Toby was jolted out of his eye-lock with the woman by the sound of a window shattering behind him. He turned to see Strobe reaching in and unlocking one of the vehicles—a Hummer—which had been parked outside the gate.

"Let's go!" Strobe yelled as he slid behind the wheel and leaned down to hot-wire the SUV.

When Toby looked back at the woman, she was walking slowly away from the fence. Her casual dismissal of him was somehow more intimidating than those feral eyes of hers. Such an odd, unexpected change in attitude!

Toby heard the Hummer roar to life behind him. When he arrived at the vehicle, Annabel was already in the passenger seat. She looked drained and unsettled from her kidnapping ordeal.

"Definitely time to book outta here," Strobe said. As he swung the Hummer around, Toby glanced back at Farrior's house. The entire compound on the other side of the gate had fallen eerily quiet. The woman, and the two men Toby had stopped with his crossbow, were nowhere in sight. There was no sign of anyone in the house.

After Strobe had turned out of the driveway and was gunning the Hummer for all it was worth down the two-lane road, Annabel looked back at Toby, then at Strobe. "Thanks, guys. I don't know what I would have done without you."

Toby was concerned for Annabel. Her eyes were clouded with emotion. He'd never seen her like this before.

"We're not out of the woods just yet, Annabel," Strobe observed. "But, hey—I'm sure you'll return the favor. One of these days."

■ ■ ■

The reason the trio couldn't see anyone in the house or on the grounds was because they were all upstairs, crowded in and around the third-story room where Annabel had been held prisoner.

A group of Farrior's inner circle was in the room, standing and kneeling around his inert body. Strobe had hit him with two blasts from the CSG. He wasn't dead. But he was stunned—practically to the point of coma.

But Alpha Man didn't go down for the count easily. When his hand twitched, a ripple of relief ran through the guttata pack. When his eyes opened, they were already clear and focused. Farrior's disciples backed away from their leader. They knew what was about to happen.

First it was the hands, the fingers growing to three times their normal length, the perfect nails turning into ugly, curved talons.

Then the feet, the long, deadly, taloned toes punching through Farrior's gorgeous suede loafers.

His chest swelled, shredding his silk shirt, the tough, reptile-like skin emerging from beneath the beautiful fabric.

His skull began to expand in strange, unexpected directions, like something being boiled, overheated.

His legs grew to an enormous length, instantly adding killer steroid-like bulk, the incredibly muscular thighs and calves obliterating his expensive trousers.

It was a bizarre, fascinating display of supernatural power. It was as though Farrior's beautiful exterior was splitting open to allow his true nature to emerge from deadly depths.

Yes, the time had finally come. The battle that had been brewing was at hand.

The monster was coming out to play.

11

Strobe was on his cell phone, talking to Harvey.

". . . of course it was risky, but what'd you expect us to do? Just sit around? We pulled it off, didn't we?" Strobe shook his head in annoyance as he listened to Harvey. "Right, right. Great. See ya soon." Pocketing the cell phone, Strobe concentrated on driving along the dark two-lane road. "Reinforcements on the way, people."

"Harvey wasn't too happy with us taking matters into our own hands, huh?" Toby said from the backseat.

"He's just ticked we managed to do something *he* wanted to do. Let's face it. Harvey's a weird guy. But he did say he was happy we were able to get you free of Farrior, Annabel."

"Like you said, though, Strobe . . . we're not out of the woods just yet." Toby looked at the towering pine trees that formed an imposing wall on either side of the road. Even though the trio had just been informed that Harvey and his troops were heading in their direction, there was no sense of celebration in the car.

Strobe stole glances in his rearview mirror as he drove. Annabel had her eyes locked on her side mirror. Toby stared out the back window. All were clearly concerned that someone might be following them.

It wasn't Farrior that Strobe and Annabel were worried about, however. It was the rest of his tribe. Would *they* come after them?

As for Toby, he couldn't get the woman's ominous warning—*You have no idea what you're dealing with here, little man*—out of his head.

"Hey!" Toby suddenly called out. "You see that?!"

"What?" Strobe asked.

Toby slid over to his side window, opened it, and craned his neck outside to get a better view of the patch of sky that wasn't obscured by the towering pine trees. "Something up above the trees. Something big."

"Still there?"

"No."

An uneasy silence filled the car as Toby and Annabel scanned the sky overhead.

"So . . ." Toby said cautiously. "You sure you killed Farrior, or what?"

"Nobody could have survived a double blast from that CSG."

Strobe slowed down to negotiate a hairpin turn. After straightening out the wheel he frowned, then leaned forward, squinting, as though a foot closer to the windshield might help him see farther down the road. "Check it out," he said. His voice was a low, concerned whisper.

Toby slid away from the side window to see what Strobe was talking about. A dark form loomed ahead, right in the middle of the road.

"What *is* that?" Toby asked.

Strobe hit the high beams to illuminate whatever it was that was blocking their way out of Echo Lake.

"Oh, my God," Annabel said softly.

All three went deadly silent as they got their first good look at an Alpha Male guttata. The monster that Farrior had become was more than simply a giant version of Sammy. Hideous in the extreme, the creature looked like the very *essence* of evil.

Staring at the beast, Toby felt numb. It was the monster from his nightmare! He had never been able to get a good look at the thing as it bore down on him in his dream landscape. Well, there it was, every terrifying feature harshly illuminated in the Hummer's head-lights. Toby's eyes were especially drawn to the enormous talons that glinted at the end of the creature's extended, muscular fingers.

Suddenly, the creature held its arms up high.

WHOOOOOOSH!!!

Like a magician's trick, a set of wings burst from the beast's body!

"Gun it, Strobe!" Toby yelled. "Blow that thing off the road!"

That's what Strobe had in mind. But as he punched the accelerator the creature rose up to an even taller height and let out an ungodly roar! It was *challenging* Strobe to ram him!

At the last second—

Strobe twisted the wheel and went off road!

Barely making it between two pine trees, Strobe cut a zigzag path through the forest maze that threatened to stop the Hummer cold, yanking the wheel back and forth as he went.

The headlight beams jerked up and down as the vehicle bounced over the uneven terrain. One of the side mirrors snapped off when it hit a thick tree trunk. The Hummer shuddered violently when it sideswiped another massive tree.

And then . . . the trees disappeared. The forest had been cleared for passage, but dangerous trunks—cut off a few feet from the ground—still remained. The high beams illuminated a dirt road ahead, running perpendicular to Strobe's path.

"Hold tight!" Strobe called out. He made a 45-degree adjustment and cut across the cleared forest toward the road.

BAM!!!

A front tire hit an exposed tree trunk. The jarring impact caused the entire right side of the Hummer to lift dangerously off the ground. The vehicle was now rolling downhill on two wheels!

Everyone instinctively threw their weight to the right side of the Hummer. The SUV continued its balancing act for another ten yards, then slammed back down on all four tires.

Suddenly, the Hummer was on the dirt road, the back tires skidding crazily, the now disintegrated front tire flopping and threatening to come off altogether.

"Look!" Toby called out from the backseat.

A football-field length ahead, the creature was coming in for a landing. Wings outspread, it hit the dirt road, pulled up, and came to a sudden stop. Once again, the Alpha guttata was blocking the trio's passage.

"Grab the backpacks, you two," Strobe ordered. "We go on three!"

"What's that supposed to mean?" Toby asked.

"We're not gonna be in the car when it smashes into that thing! Ready? *One . . .* "

There was no protest from Annabel or Toby. Toby tossed one of the backpacks to Annabel and grabbed the other one.

"Where's the CSG?" Toby yelled.

"Thing only had three charges," Strobe called back.

Bad news. They would have to face the creature with just their crossbows. And their wits. But first they would have to survive their leap from the car.

"Two . . ."

The Hummer barreled toward the beast. It didn't look like it was budging. Toby had time for one final thought as he opened the rear door and braced for his jump:

THIS IS NUTS!!!!!

"THREE!"

The forest exploded with a crazy quilt of sound and

action as Strobe, Annabel, and Toby leaped from the car. . . .

The Hummer crashed into the creature like a metallic battering ram. . . .

The trio rolled and bounced on the dirt road. . . .

The creature was slammed to the ground from the force of the impact. . . .

The Hummer flipped over and over in spectacular fashion, finally sliding to an upside-down halt at the side of the road.

And then . . . just like that . . .

Silence.

A cloud of dust, kicked up from flying bodies and the levitating Hummer, hovered in the air, wrapping itself around the landscape like a transparent shroud. A cough erupted from somewhere in the woods.

"Annabel? Toby?" Strobe was the first one to stagger to his feet. Fortunately, a bank of dirt on either side of the road had slightly cushioned their leap from the car. Annabel was just on the other side of the bank, across the road from Strobe. She sat up cautiously as Strobe ran over to her. "You okay?"

"I think so." Annabel was obviously dazed. "No broken bones, anyway, from the feel of it."

"You rest for a moment. I'll find Toby."

He was on the other side of the road from Annabel, tangled up in a stand of wild gooseberry bushes. Good thing he'd landed in the bushes. The ground fell off sharply just on the other side of them. Scratched and bloodied, Toby was separating himself from some clinging branches when Strobe appeared from the cloudy haze that still hung over the road.

"Annabel okay?" Toby asked.

Strobe nodded yes.

"You don't look so good," Toby observed. Strobe's right arm hung limply at his side, a telltale result of his leap from the Hummer.

"Neither do you," Strobe said as Toby hobbled away from the bushes, favoring his left leg.

"Strobe!" Annabel called out. Strobe and Toby hustled back to the road. Annabel was standing unsteadily, staring at an incredible sight.

The creature was back up on two feet!

The upside-down Hummer's high beams—still on and pointed at the beast—lent a dramatic, backlit glow to the scene in the middle of the road. Still dazed from its up-close-and-personal meeting with the Hummer, the creature was nonetheless shaking off the dust and getting ready to resume its battle with the trio.

"Can't believe he survived that," Toby whispered in awe.

The creature's head swiveled at the sound of Toby's voice, its eyes locking on to the trio.

That was all Strobe needed to see.

"Rrrrrunnnnn!"

Toby and Annabel grabbed their backpacks and followed Strobe into the woods. Coming to the steep incline just beyond the bushes that had caught Toby, Strobe took off down the hill in a sitting position. Annabel and Toby were right behind him.

After a wild slide down the dirt-and-pine-needled incline—a dusty variation of an amusement park water ride—they came to an abrupt halt at the bottom. Stretched out in front of them was a large construction site, covering acres and acres of prime Echo Lake real estate.

In the dark it looked like an alien landscape. Stark, skeletal frames rose up from concrete pads. Bins of overflowing refuse dotted the area, looking somehow threatening in the pitch-black darkness. Large drainage pipes twisted around the grounds, resembling some kind of giant, fossilized, prehistoric snake.

Strobe hopped to his feet and ran toward the site, passing a sign at the entrance to the complex:

ECHO LAKE ESTATES

LUXURY HOMES BY THE LAKE

CONTRACTOR: FARRIOR & ASSOCIATES

Annabel stayed close to the limping Toby as she scanned the sky overhead, keeping a watch for the creature. Strobe chose a structure that had a completed wooden exterior and gaping window and door holes for their shelter. He waited at the entrance for Annabel and Toby to arrive, gave the area a quick once-over, then disappeared inside.

The trio found a place in the center of the house to collapse. Backs against a stack of plywood, their quick, heaving intakes of breath echoed back at them from the stark walls of the room.

"So . . ." Toby said finally. He didn't finish his thought, whatever it was.

More silence. Heavy breathing.

"Okay . . . well . . ." Strobe said. Then, "I didn't have anything planned for tonight, anyway."

"I have three words for the two of you," Annabel said.

Toby and Strobe were instantly curious. *Three words?*

"This's a problem?" Toby guessed.

"That's four words," Strobe pointed out.

"No. *This's*." Toby spelled the word for Strobe.

"That's not a proper contraction."

"I think it might be."

"It isn't."

"Doesn't matter," Annabel interjected. "Those aren't the three words, anyway."

Strobe thought for a moment, then said, "Lemme outta here!" He gave Annabel a look that asked, *Is that it?*

Toby frowned. "That's *five* words."

"No, it isn't." Strobe spelled "lemme" and "outta" for Toby.

"No way, Strobe. If you're not giving me 'this's,' I'm not giving you 'lemme' and 'outta.'"

"Okay, boys! That's enough!" Strobe and Toby continued to glare at each other. "It's depressor dens inferioris. Okay? Those are the three words."

"No way can we get at that thing's DDI," Strobe said.

"We have to. It's the only way to kill it."

"Wait, wait, wait a second!" Toby said, suddenly excited. "We're at a construction site! There must be some kind of explosives around here. We'll blow the monster up!"

"Now *that's* a thought," Strobe said.

"I don't like it," Annabel countered. "We'd have to run around the site to see what we can find. We'd be open targets."

Toby thought about that, then gave Annabel a grudging nod. "Maybe we can hold this thing off until Harvey and the troops get here," he suggested. Strobe and Annabel both looked skeptical at that idea. "Yeah, no, I don't think so, either."

Suddenly—

A sound! The three immediately tensed. As their eyes darted from one window opening to the next, several deer scurried past one of the windows. Everyone exhaled in relief.

"Next time it might not be something so friendly," Annabel said. "We'd better figure out what we're doing. *Fast.*"

"Okay," Strobe said. "You two suit up. Annabel, you can use my arm and leg plates. And my crossbow. I'm no good with my shoulder. I wouldn't be able to hit the side of one of these houses with an arrow."

"What are you saying?" Annabel asked.

"That you're right. It's the DDI or nothing. I'll be the

guinea pig. Alpha Man has to have something to strike at, right?"

"No way," Annabel said adamantly.

"You have a better idea?"

"Yeah. A decoy of some sort. Make the creature *think* he's striking at one of us."

"What, you mean like some kind of dummy? A scarecrow kind of thing?"

"It's worth a try. Guttata see shapes, not detail. In the dark, it might not know the difference."

"It'll know. There'll be no scent."

"There will be if the dummy's wearing your T-shirt," Toby pointed out. "Believe me, that thing has a scent."

Strobe looked at Toby for a moment, then stood up, took off his T-shirt, and threw it in Toby's face. "Okay. Let's see what we can rig up."

■ ■ ■

After strapping on his arm and leg plates and getting his crossbow ready, Toby joined Strobe upstairs to help scavenge for decoy parts.

"So, anyway, when did you learn how to hot-wire a car?" Toby asked as he surveyed a large room through his NVGs.

"That's a pretty random question," Strobe said from the nearby closet.

"Just nervous talk. Was it when you were twelve? Is that how you stole that car?"

"Somehow I don't think now's the time or place to talk about my questionable past."

"Right. Anyhow, that little skill of yours came in pretty handy tonight."

"Too bad it was just a temporary solution." Strobe held up some wire that he had found. "I'm gonna take this down to Annabel."

"Be right there."

Annabel looked up from her work when she saw Strobe coming down the stairs. "Get what I need?" When Strobe handed her the wire, she tied one end to the main support of the scarecrow they had constructed.

Strobe stood, watching Annabel. She had been unusually subdued after her escape from the monster pit. But as she worked on the decoy, Annabel looked focused and intense. Galvanized. Strobe was happy to see that her reliable spirit had returned. She did a double take when she noticed that Strobe hadn't moved. "Everything all right?" she asked.

"You bet. Ready to go."

"Good. When Toby gets down here, we'll be on our way." Annabel double-checked the strength of the decoy.

"So, anyway . . ." Strobe said.

Annabel looked over the shoulder of the wooden figure at Strobe.

"I was thinking . . . if everything goes okay here? We get out of this?"

Annabel nodded.

"I thought maybe you, me, and Toby could go rafting."

That was obviously the last thing Annabel expected to hear. "Rafting?"

"Yeah. There's this place called Ohiopyle. I checked it out online. Looks pretty good. You ever do that? Rafting?"

"No, but I've always wanted to."

"Well, what do you think?"

Annabel was definitely confused by Strobe's offer. Why was he asking her this now?

"It'd be fun," Strobe pointed out. "Besides, maybe it'd give us some time to . . . talk."

"You want to go rafting and talk?"

Strobe smiled at the way that sounded. "Something like that."

Whether or not Strobe's invitation had anything to do with the night they were on their mostly silent stake-out together, Annabel wasn't sure. But she did sense that what was going on here was kind of a delicate thing.

"Yes, I would like to go rafting with you and Toby, Strobe."

"Terrific."

Even though she was standing close to Strobe, Annabel could barely see him in the dark room.

"Well . . . I better go check on our guy."

Watching Strobe go back up to the second floor, Annabel shook her head in surprise. What an unexpected thing just happened!

But there was no time to dwell on it. There was still a trap to prepare for the Thing That Wouldn't Die.

■ ■ ■

"Now!" Annabel commanded.

She and Toby burst from the house and ran for the concrete pipe near the curb. They scrambled inside and crawled through the circular tunnel until they had reached the end of the line of pipe. They were now looking at the backyard of the house across the street from their "shelter" house.

Annabel checked the sky for the creature. "Clear," she said, then sprinted from the pipe, across the yard, and into the house through the gaping back door. Toby was close behind. The two made their way through the kitchen area, down a hall, and into one of the rooms at the front of the house. Taking position at an open window that provided a clear view of their house across the street, they quickly loaded their weapons.

"All set, Strobe," Annabel said into her headset when she and Toby were ready.

"Okay," Strobe replied. "Ready or not, the twin I never knew I had is about to make his appearance."

Sighting along his crossbow shaft, Toby watched as Strobe positioned the decoy in the middle of the front door entrance. The crude skeleton of wood, wire, and metal rebar scavenged from the house had been given the final touch of Strobe's T-shirt.

That's not gonna work! Toby thought when he saw the decoy. It looked so ridiculous, Toby practically laughed out loud. Especially when the decoy started to twitch back and forth, the result of Strobe manipulating the wire Annabel had tied to the frame.

As the decoy across the way continued its come-on dance, Toby now had more than just a giggle or two to try to stifle. He could feel the unmistakable, totally inappropriate rumblings of a laughing jag coming on!

"Toby?" Annabel whispered when she saw Toby's shaking shoulders. "What's wrong?"

Toby was dismayed to find that he couldn't answer Annabel's question. He was losing it! He was having a meltdown! That's what this was, Toby realized. All of the death-defying escapades had finally gotten to him.

"Toby," Annabel said, the concern apparent in her voice.

"He's comin'!" Strobe warned from across the street.

That sobered Toby up like a shot. A slap to the face couldn't have done a better job.

SLAM!!!

Startled by the sight of the creature's monstrous tenfoot frame hitting the ground in front of Strobe's yawning front door, Toby almost accidently set off his crossbow. Again. Quickly composing himself, he locked the creature in the sights of his powerful crossbow scope. The thing was standing statue-still, sizing up the decoy in the doorway.

"Take the bait," Annabel whispered as she and Toby

zeroed in on the all-important area at the back of the creature's neck. The DDI.

The beast suddenly took a step toward the decoy. Toby and Annabel pressed their fingers delicately up against their crossbow triggers and waited for their shot.

"Almost there . . ." Annabel said.

And then—

Yes! There it was! The DDI's protective covering had lifted!

WHOOOOSH!!!

Toby blinked his eyes. What just happened? He looked over the top of his crossbow. The creature was gone! It was as though it had simply disappeared!

But when Toby looked up, there it was, flying off into the darkness. The thousand-pound beast was so powerful it had been able to take off like a rocket!

"Damn!" Strobe said over the duo's headsets.

The trio was stunned at how quickly their grand plan had dissolved into failure. After a moment of frustrated silence, Strobe said, "We may have to go after those explosives after all, Tobe."

CRASH!!!

Toby and Annabel jumped in surprise. They looked up at the ceiling. Something had landed on their roof!

"Strobe?" Annabel whispered into her headset.

"Yeah, he's up there."

Suddenly, a large, dark shape shot past overhead and dive-bombed directly toward Strobe's hideout!

"Strobe!" Annabel called out.

The creature exploded through the front door, smashed the decoy, and splintered part of the frame as it disappeared inside the house. Toby was frozen at the sight. The thing had attacked! It was inside the house with Strobe!

Annabel leaped though the window frame and raced across the yard. When Toby tried to follow Annabel, his T-shirt caught on an exposed frame nail and jerked him back. He ripped loose and ran to catch up with his fleet-footed partner. Before he made it to the sidewalk, she had already disappeared into the house.

Hideous sounds echoed from inside the hollow structure. Roars from the creature. Glass shattering. Wood splintering.

Just as Toby was about to enter the house, Annabel and Strobe appeared from a side door, charged across the backyard, and took shelter inside a tunnel of concrete pipe. They had escaped the creature's attack!

But the thing was more than ready to take the battle outside. With a concussively powerful roar, it flashed into view from behind the house and went after the line of pipe where Annabel and Strobe were hiding.

Toby dashed behind a trash bin and tried to get a bead on the creature with his crossbow. It wasn't easy. The thing was a fast-moving target as it tossed aside sections of the heavy concrete pipe as though they were weightless.

Toby suddenly felt powerless. How on earth could he possibly help his friends with just a crossbow? The beast looked like a guttata Terminator as it demolished Strobe and Annabel's flimsy shelter—bit by concrete bit.

Don't think! Toby's brain screamed. *Shoot!!!*

Toby took aim and squeezed the trigger. When the arrow struck the creature's back shoulder, the thing stopped its rampage, flicked the annoying arrow out of its leathery skin, and looked in Toby's direction with a ferocious frown.

Toby aimed and fired again.

AAAAAAAAARRRRRRRRRR!!!!

Toby was shocked to hear the creature roar out in

pain. But then he saw what had happened. His second arrow had lodged in the beast's eye! The injured Alpha let out another howl of rage, grabbed Toby's arrow, and yanked it from its eye socket. Yellow blood—looking sickly white, pus-like in the monotone night—streamed down its face from the wound.

Toby recoiled from the disgusting sight. Then he froze. The creature had just focused its one good eye on Toby's trash-bin hiding place. It knew where the second arrow had come from!

But this is just what Toby had wanted to do. Distract the creature from Strobe and Annabel. Now what? One word rocketed through Toby's brain:

Retreat!

Flinging the crossbow strap over his shoulder, Toby turned and bolted across the street.

As soon as the creature saw Toby, it pushed off from the ground and flew after him with a powerful thrust of its wings.

Toby scampered through the house where he and Annabel had fired their arrows and bolted out the rear entrance. He had no idea where he was going. All he knew was that he had to outrun the Alpha. Somehow.

Huffing toward another house, Toby looked back over his shoulder. The creature was quickly gaining on him.

But something was wrong with it. It looked wobbly—slightly off balance—as it flew. Apparently Toby's arrow had done some damage.

Advantage: Toby. That didn't make him feel much better. Desperately hopscotching from one house to the next in an attempt to stay one step ahead of his pursuer, Toby's mind raced faster than his legs.

Where to go? What to do? With no plan, Toby was just riffing. And running for his life.

Suddenly, a glimpse of water between the skeletal frame of a nearby house. Echo Lake. Toby changed course. He wasn't sure why, but water seemed to be his salvation. He was halfway through another partially completed house when—

SLAM!!!

The creature hit the ground not ten yards from the house, blocking Toby's exit out the rear door! Toby skidded to a stop. The stitches of his wound had come loose and blood was seeping through his cargo shorts. The beast sniffed hungrily when it caught the scent of Toby's blood. It smashed through the door frame—a rude entrance into the house—and reached out a long, leathery hand to reel Toby in.

Toby dove away from the creature, rolled a few yards, leaped to his feet, and scrambled through a nearby doorway. The thing was right behind him. But it was too large to follow Toby through the narrow opening.

CRACK!!! CRACK!!! CRACK!!!

The powerful beast ripped the framing around the door to shreds and dove after its prey. Sharp talons cut deep grooves in the wooden floor as the creature pounded down the hallway. By the time it smashed into the room at the end of the corridor . . .

Toby was gone. He had crawled through a window and was racing for the lake.

Toby looked back to see the beast emerge from a gaping hole it had just created in the side of the house. Leaping over a pile of metal rebar poles, Toby ran as fast as his throbbing legs would carry him toward a nearby pier that reached out into Echo Lake.

Behind him, the creature had gone airborne again. It flew only a few feet above the ground, its one cyclops eye locked on to Toby's bobbing back.

This was it! It was going in for the kill!

Twenty yards . . . ten . . . five . . .

Pounding across the wooden planks of the pier, Toby had the bizarre, out-of-body thought that he would be waking up any time now. But of course he wouldn't be. This was his nightmare come true. The sharp sting of pain from the Alpha's talons would come any second now!

Toby made a snap decision to dive off the side of the pier instead of racing to the end where the water was deepest. He hit the black water with a loud splash and disappeared underwater just as the Alpha swooped down and grabbed for him. The creature instantly pulled up, hovered over the lake, and waited for its prey to reappear.

Beneath the lake's surface, Toby was swimming as deep as his lungs would allow him to go. He couldn't see an inch in front of his face. The water was shockingly cold. When he couldn't hold his breath any longer, he pushed upward for a gulp of air. As soon as his head broke above the lake's surface, the creature's dark shape dropped toward him!

Toby took a quick breath and retreated back underwater. As he did, the beast's reaching talons slashed him across the back. Toby winced at the pain, but he kept pushing for the lake's floor. As much as *that* hurt, Toby knew it was nothing compared to what the creature would do to him the next time he went up for air. Or the time after that.

It was the Alpha guttata that had time on its side, after all. It could stay airborne for as long as it wanted. Toby's energy was draining quickly, however. He simply couldn't wait to go up for air much longer.

As he desperately held his breath, Toby's oxygen-deprived brain began to urge him to give up the fight. It would be so simple. Just float to the surface and let the creature have at him. The longer Toby stayed underwater, the better that idea sounded.

But then, the adrenaline blast of a possibly life-saving idea jolted the boy back into action.

The pier!

If Toby could make it under the pier, that just might save him. He could stay beneath the wooden structure—treading water and breathing all the air he needed—and the creature wouldn't be able to get to him. Unless it started ripping up the planks, which Toby wouldn't put past the insane beast.

But Toby was willing to take that chance. It was better than blindly going to the surface time after time.

So Toby swam in what he thought was the direction

of the pier, hoping he could make it before having to go back to the surface for another gulp of air. Because he knew Alpha Man would be there. Waiting for him. Ready to take his revenge.

An eye for an eye, after all.

12

In his mad dash to stay one step in front of the creature, Toby hadn't had time to think about Annabel and Strobe.

But they were thinking about Toby. After their close call inside the pipe, Annabel and Strobe had looked out to see the thing flying away from them. Then they had spotted Toby, limping from one house to the next.

That's when they gave chase.

Annabel had led the way, her crossbow bouncing against her back as she ran. She and Strobe had watched as Toby leaped into the lake. Then the creature's attempt to snatch him from the water when he resurfaced.

Now they were flattened against the side of a large recreational building near the entrance to the pier. In contrast to the houses surrounding it, this structure was complete. It was like a sparkling jewel for the high-end development, a showcase to whet the appetites of potential buyers.

One of these days the building would be the center of lighthearted activity. Bands playing. People dancing. A nice dinner, perhaps, overlooking the lake.

One of these days.

Annabel sighted along the shaft of her crossbow. Strobe stood next to her, weaponless, but ready to help in any way that he could. With a final aim at the creature, still hovering over the water and waiting for Toby's reappearance, Annabel fired.

The arrow slammed into the beast's skin, a sensitive area near the left wing. Whirling in midair, the Alpha instantly zeroed in on the recreational building, flew toward it, glided over the top, and landed with a thud on the other side.

No sign of Annabel and Strobe.

Creeeeeeeak.

The creature's head swung in the direction of the building's double French-door entrance, which had suddenly swung open. Annabel and Strobe had taken shelter inside! Two quick strides and the thing was at the door. With a savage roar, the creature went ballistic on the entrance. It *ate it* right up!

Chunks of wood went flying. Glass shattered. Within moments the beast had created a huge gap in the side of the building. It pushed its way inside to go after Annabel and Strobe.

Good thing they weren't actually in there.

As soon as Annabel had fired her crossbow she tossed a sweaty armband through the open door of the building—a hopeful diversion—and ran with Strobe to hide behind a nearby construction trailer.

That's where they were now, listening to the out-of-control creature crash through the interior of the building. Suddenly, a section of wall exploded and the beast reappeared, nostrils flaring as it angrily scanned the area for its prey.

"Wow," Strobe said, completely awed at the Alpha's over-the-top power.

"What do we do, Strobe?" Annabel asked. Her concern was constricting her throat, making her voice raspy. "Any idea how we can stop this thing?"

Strobe's silence answered Annabel's question. From the looks of it, they had run out of options. The creature was like a demonic battering ram, able to pulverize anything that got in its path. There didn't appear to be any possible way to get rid of the thing.

But there was one thing Strobe and Annabel hadn't counted on.

Crazy Toby.

■ ■ ■

He had waited until his lungs felt like they were disintegrating inside his chest before he had returned to the water's surface.

When he discovered that he hadn't made it under the pier—it was a few feet away—Toby instantly panicked. He was certain the creature would get him this time, would snatch him up in its taloned feet!

But then Toby saw the thing demolishing the recreational building. He quickly put two and two together, figured his friends had followed him and tried to help in some way, and were now trapped inside the disintegrating shell of wood, metal, and glass.

As Toby treaded water and watched the creature disappear inside the building, a blinding flash of anger suddenly blazed inside him.

"HEY!" he heard himself yell. Swimming to shore and pulling himself from the water, Toby had the strange sensation that his limbs and voice were being controlled by something outside his body. *"What the hell you think you're doin'?!"*

When the creature reappeared from the building, Toby picked up a rock, ran a few feet, and launched it. The rock found its mark, but bounced harmlessly off of the creature's leg. Once again, however, Toby had gotten its attention. The beast turned to look at Toby as he strode in its direction.

Behind the trailer, Annabel and Strobe stared at Toby in shocked disbelief.

"What's he doing?" Annabel asked.

"He's snapped, man. He's totally snapped."

Actually, Strobe was pretty much on the mark with that observation. The stress, the craziness of the situation, his pain, his concern for his friends . . . it was all suddenly just *too much* for Toby. Any sense of logic, of self-preservation, of caution, had simply vanished from his head. The only thing left was a blinding anger and, really, a kind of temporary insanity.

"What *right* do you have to do this? *HUH?!*" Toby was now about twenty yards from the creature, which stared at him as he approached. The beast's prey was always wildly panicked, totally blinded by fear. It could *smell* that fear on its victims. But the helpless human, yelling at the top of his lungs, gave off no scent of fear or panic. The Alpha looked, if not confused, at least curious at the sight of Toby as he continued to walk in its direction.

"You pick on a defenseless girl like Chelsea Travers! Take away Mrs. Child's only son! Go after my friends!! *I won't let this stand!!* Got it? This is where it stops! You worthless, ugly-as-sin, unholy, good-for-nothing *PIECE OF CRAP!!!*"

Toby suddenly froze in his tracks. It was as though the air had been sucked right out of him. Then . . . looking like he was returning from some kind of hypnotic spell, Toby's eyes slowly focused on the monster in front of him. His expression was one of total surprise. *What had he just done?!!!*

Instantly catching a whiff of Toby's return jolt of fear, the creature opened its gargantuan mouth and screamed, the force of its roar literally causing Toby's hair to ripple, as though blown by a sudden breeze!

Move, man! MOVE!!

That's what Toby's brain desperately urged him to do, but his legs wouldn't budge. He felt like he was frozen in place. He didn't think he could move if his life depended on it.

Hey, wait a second. It did!

But it was too late to run. The creature was already

coming at Toby like a freight train. It was about to take his head clean off with a snip of its razor-sharp teeth, when—

Strobe dove out of the darkness and tackled his friend!

The beast's jaws snapped shut where Toby had just stood, finding air instead of flesh.

Strobe jumped up, grabbed a rod of rebar lying nearby, and went at the creature, using the metal shaft like a spear.

The beast stepped back to avoid Strobe's weapon. It parried with a slash of its talons. Strobe ducked and attacked again.

The furious back-and-forth battle lasted only a few seconds. The creature easily avoided one of Strobe's lunges and retaliated with a vicious swipe of its long arm.

The force of the beast's blow lifted Strobe from the ground and sent him flying. He hit the ground awkwardly, his right leg and arm bent beneath him. Strobe clutched his already bad arm and yelled out in pain.

"Strobe!"

Toby ran over and grabbed Strobe across the chest. He slowly pulled him away from the creature as it closed in on the two of them. He was trying to get back in the water. Under the pier.

"Don't be stupid, man. Get outta here," Strobe ordered.

"No way."

"*Go!* I mean it!"

"No way I'm leavin' you!"

Glancing over his shoulder, Toby knew he would not be able to make it to the water. He grabbed the rod of rebar that had been knocked from Strobe's hand, came around, and stood in front of Strobe to shield him from the creature. When the monstrous guttata was close enough, Toby lunged with the metal shaft.

The Alpha slapped Toby onto his back as though he were a mere toy. Knocked practically senseless by the Alpha's casual smackdown, Toby could hardly move, let alone get away from the thing. Still, he desperately tried to inch away from the beast as it took another menacing step toward him.

Long strings of saliva dripped from the Alpha's mouth. Its finger talons snapped together, as though sharpening themselves for a bit of flesh carving. Huge black-veined wings curved up and over Toby, like a death shroud.

This was it! The final, decisive attack! Toby knew he couldn't dream his way out of this one. The creature rose up and prepared to rip into him, when suddenly—

ZZZZZZAP!

The beast's one good eye shot wide open in shock. The thing looked like it had been hit with a sudden jolt of electricity. Toby stared at the creature, not quite believing what he was seeing. But what *was* he seeing? What just happened?

Toby watched, fascinated, as the Alpha guttata's surprised expression was suddenly replaced by . . .

Nothing.

The spark of life in the mighty beast's hideous frame had vanished. The creature stood upright for a moment, then slowly toppled forward. Toby had to roll away to avoid getting flattened by the monster's tonnage.

The thing slammed to the ground with incredible force. Sure enough, protruding from the back of its neck, was an arrow.

Annabel stood thirty or so yards away, still sighting along the shaft of her crossbow. She stood like that for a moment, then slowly brought the weapon down and held it at her side.

Dazed disbelief all around. Just like that, it was over! The creature was dead! It didn't seem possible!

Toby and Strobe were too exhausted to get to their feet, let alone celebrate, so they both stayed right where they were as Annabel walked toward them. Strobe let out a relieved laugh. "Oh, *man*," was all he could think of to say.

Toby smiled. But Annabel wasn't smiling. She was way too concerned for her boys. "I've never seen anyone actually fly through the air like that, Strobe."

"You should have seen it from my perspective." Strobe tried to move, but quickly stopped with a wince. Something was definitely wrong with his leg as well as his arm.

"Just . . . take it easy," Annabel instructed as she knelt next to him.

Strobe watched Annabel closely as she inspected his leg. "I didn't think you'd be so quick about it." Annabel wasn't sure what Strobe meant by that. "You already saved us back," he explained.

Annabel smiled. "I guess that makes us even."

"For now, anyway."

As Annabel found a piece of wood and pulled a bandage from her backpack to fashion a splint for Strobe's injured leg, Toby heaved a sigh of relief and exhaustion and lay back on the grass. He closed his eyes and soaked in the wonderful feeling of just being *alive*.

His hyper mind whirled, grabbing and discarding one electric image of the battle with the Alpha after another, then something started to muscle its way into the series of action snapshots in Toby's mind, something indistinct at first, but then there it was in bold letters and it was the only thing Toby was thinking of.

Evil cannot see good, but good can always see evil.

G vs E. The never-ending battle.

Tonight, Toby knew, good had definitely seen evil. It had looked the beast right in the eye . . . and had triumphed.

EPILOGUE:
GRADUATION

"...in recognition of your completion of the KP Training Program, I declare you, Annabel Oshiro, Gordon Tibbles, and Toby Magill official Killer Pizza MCOs."

The three new graduates stood with Harvey and Steve at the front of the Killer Pizza classroom. Strobe shifted uncomfortably on his crutches. He wished he could get at that itch under his cast.

"Seeing as this is a secret organization," Harvey continued, "you will not receive any kind of badge or certificate. But know that you are a member of an elite force. It is something to be proud of. There is much more to learn, of course, and I hope that you will continue to study, continue to protect and serve your community from the dark forces that exist in this world for many years to come."

Harvey shook each of their hands, then Steve did the same.

"When do we get those raises?" Strobe asked.

Annabel rolled her eyes. She couldn't believe that was the first thing Strobe thought to ask after being officially declared an MCO.

Harvey didn't seem to mind the question. "As promised, today," he replied. Then he gave the trio his version of a smile and left the classroom.

"That's it?" Strobe asked in surprise.

"That's it," Steve echoed.

"We don't get a cake or anything like that?"

"No. However . . ." Steve pulled three envelopes from his pocket and gave one each to Strobe, Annabel, and Toby. "I'm more than happy to hand out your bonuses for extracurricular activities taken on during your training program."

Strobe ripped open his envelope and pulled out a small stack of crisp twenties. "Hey, this isn't bad. I'll take it."

"Once again, congratulations," Steve said as he gave everyone a warm smile. "Now if you'll excuse me, I have some packing to do."

Anxious to get back to New York, Harvey and Steve

were leaving that night. Which meant that the new MCOs would be in charge of the Hidden Hills branch of Killer Pizza's underground organization of monster hunters.

After Steve left, Strobe looked around the classroom. "Still feels kind of anticlimactic, don't you think?"

"What'd you expect?" Annabel asked. "A marching band? Cheerleaders?"

"That would've been nice. After all, it's not like we're gonna be shipped off to some monster hot spot halfway around the world. We're gonna be right here, waiting for the next fiend infestation. Whatever it might be."

"Poor baby," Annabel said. "Would you feel better if we had some kind of celebration? Say, Prospect Park? Sunset?"

"That's a great idea," Strobe said, immediately perking up. "I'll bring the drinks."

"I'll bring the snacks," Toby offered.

"What you can bring," Strobe said, looking at Annabel, "is me. On the back of your bike. Otherwise, I won't get there till midnight."

"You got it," Annabel said. She hung back as Strobe and Toby headed for the door.

"Comin'?" Strobe asked. Annabel didn't move. Just looked at Strobe with a mischievous grin. "What's that look for?"

No reply.

"What's with you? What is it?"

"Your name is Gordon Tibbles?"

"Yeah? So?"

Annabel's smile grew wider as she walked past Strobe on her way to the door.

"Hold on!" Strobe ordered. "What's wrong with Gordon Tibbles?"

"It ain't Strobe, that's for sure," Annabel said over her shoulder as she left the room.

Strobe glared at Toby, as though daring him to make fun of his name, as well, then lurched after Annabel on his crutches.

■ ■ ■

It was a beautiful evening. Perfect temperature. No humidity. Toby was already at the park when Strobe and Annabel arrived. He was sitting on the bench, looking at the neighborhood below. There were more kids than usual playing in the streets. More adults sitting on their white plastic chairs, arranged in semicircles on their lush lawns, talking to the neighbors.

The people weren't out because they now felt safer, knowing that a pack of guttata had exited their city after the death of their leader. Nobody down below had a clue about that, of course. No, they were groovin' on the evening because they all shared the same instinctive feeling.

Summer's almost over. Time to enjoy it while it's still here!

"Hey, guys," Toby said when he saw Strobe and Annabel approach, his heart skipping a beat at the sight of Annabel. For most of the summer, Annabel had been wearing the same black Killer Pizza T-shirt as Toby and Strobe. But tonight she had discarded the T-shirt and jeans and was wearing a very colorful tank top and miniskirt, accented by pink flip-flops. She looked absolutely gorgeous.

"Been here long?" Annabel asked as she sat next to Toby. She placed the plastic cooler she had been carrying at her feet.

"A little while," Toby replied. "Just enjoying the evening. Sittin' . . . thinkin'."

"What about?" Annabel asked.

Strobe sat heavily and tossed his crutches to the grass.

"Well, for one thing . . ." Toby pointed out an expanse of neatly trimmed grass to the right of where they were sitting. "That's Hidden Hills Cemetery over there, Strobe."

Railroad tracks cut a straight line between the residential area of Hidden Hills and the grassy area of the cemetery, which was symmetrically dotted with flat granite gravestones.

"I'm familiar with the cemetery, Tobe. I do live here, after all."

"Right. Anyway, this friend of mine? The guy with the Echo Lake house? When we were kids we would sneak across those tracks at night and tell ghost stories among the gravestones. It was a pretty scary thing to do when you're ten years old."

"Is the point of this story that you've grown up a little since then? Or now you have some *real* stories to tell?"

"Both, I guess," Toby said. Then he smiled. He was caught up in a nostalgic moment and feeling pretty good. Actually, it wasn't just nostalgia that had Toby in a good mood. Thanks to a delivery of the perfect replacement for the shredded living room sofa a few short hours before Mr. and Mrs. Magill returned from their vacation, everything was cool on the home front. The Subaru was back in the garage, as well, which meant there were no telltale signs of Toby's misadventures to indicate that anything had gone awry during the past few days.

More important though, as far as Toby's good mood went, was the fact that Chelsea was on the mend from her guttata bite. Toby had gone to the hospital earlier in the day and was thrilled to find Chelsea wide awake and sitting up in bed.

The breakthrough, the thing that had turned things around for Chelsea, was an antidote Harvey had been able to concoct from Chris Child's blood. So, if Toby hadn't been able to win his battle with Child . . .

Chelsea would never know that Toby had played an integral part in her recovery. For one thing, he would never tell her. For another, Chelsea didn't appear to have any memory of the first time Toby had come to see her in the hospital.

That was okay with Toby. *He* knew what he'd done for Chelsea. That was all the reward he needed. It was the main reason he had signed up for the academy in the first place, after all. To protect the unsuspecting public from the unknown evil that lived in their midst.

"Hey, what do you have there?" Strobe asked. He was looking at an insulated Killer Pizza delivery sleeve under the bench.

"Our snack," Toby replied, picking up the sleeve and sliding out a large pizza.

"You brought a pizza for a snack?" Strobe looked disappointed. "C'mon, Tobe."

Toby distributed a couple of slices to Strobe and Annabel.

"Try it," he said.

Annabel studied the pizza slice, then took a bite. After savoring the taste and wiping some cheese from her lip, she nodded appreciatively. "This is excellent. What is it? I don't recognize it from the menu."

"Hey, this has a *kick* to it," Strobe said after taking a nibble. "What's in this? Some kind of curry?"

"A chef never reveals his secrets."

"Wait," Annabel said. "Are you saying this is yours? Your own creation?"

Toby nodded.

"That's fantastic!"

Toby shrugged, trying not to look too pleased with himself.

"So what's in it?" Strobe pressed. "Is this curry, or what? What kind of cheese is this?"

"I'm not telling, Strobe."

"Have Harvey and Steve tasted this?" Annabel asked.

"Just yesterday they did."

"And?"

Toby didn't answer right away. He was building the moment. And thinking about the past week. After going in early to Killer Pizza—before it opened—every day to experiment with his new recipes, he'd finally cracked Dragon Breath, had finally hit on just the right combination of ingredients.

"They said I could give it a test run at the Hidden Hills branch of Killer Pizza," Toby said with a smile.

"Chef Toby!" Annabel said, giving Toby a big hug. "I'm so proud of you!" Toby smiled, basking in the moment.

"Congrats, man," Strobe said. He reached for the cooler and pulled out three soda bottles. Each one was a different, sparkling color. "I have just the thing to go with your new creation."

"Italian soda?" Toby asked.

Strobe nodded. "Direct from Italy. Compliments of my mom. I have Raspberry. Cinnamon. Almond Rock."

"Ladies first," Toby said.

Annabel chose Raspberry. Toby took the Almond Rock. The trio fell into a comfortable silence as they ate their pizza and drank their Italian sodas and looked out across the quickly darkening landscape. They were almost done with their evening celebration when Annabel's cell phone rang.

"Harvey," Annabel said after a brief conversation. "He's going on a final pass through the neighborhood in the Commando before taking off. Just to make sure everything's clear. Wants to know if we'd like to go out on our first official patrol as MCOs."

"You bet," Strobe said, instantly excited. "Who knows what the radar might turn up?" Strobe reached for his crutches, propped himself up, and careened toward the stairs.

"The man likes his work," Toby said.

"Yes, he does," Annabel said as she packed up the picnic basket.

Toby retrieved his pizza sleeve from under the bench, made sure they hadn't left anything behind, then took a final look around the park. Fireflies were starting to accent the quickly darkening hilltop area. Lights were coming on in the houses below. Magic hour.

Toby took it all in, nodded thoughtfully, then walked across the park to join Strobe and Annabel. When he caught up with them at the top of the stairs, the three new Monster Combat Officers headed off to see if anything was going bump in the Hidden Hills night.

RECIPE FOR
FIERY DRAGON'S BREATH PIZZA
(MAKES ONE TWELVE-INCH PIE/APPROX. 6 SLICES)

*Note: always ask an adult for help when working in the kitchen

INGREDIENTS:

PIZZA BASE:

You can buy one already-made pizza crust or (for the more adventurous chef) make it from scratch, using:

2 cups of flour
½ tsp salt
½ tsp fresh yeast
¾ cup lukewarm water
1 tbsp olive oil

SAUCE:

1 small onion, finely chopped
½ clove of garlic, crushed
½ tsp dried oregano
7 oz can chopped tomatoes
salt and pepper
½ tbsp olive oil

TOPPINGS:

½ roast pepper (from jar or roasted in the oven, deskinned and deseeded)
pinch of Cajun spice
½ small jalapeno pepper, deseeded and thinly sliced
½ small packet of pepperoni
½ oz freshly grated Parmesan
3 oz mozzarella, roughly chopped
a few basil or oregano leaves

DIRECTIONS:

1. In a large bowl, mix flour and salt together, dissolve yeast in water and slowly add to the flour. Mix well until it forms a dough. If too sticky, add more flour.

2. Knead the dough for roughly 10 minutes. The dough should feel smooth and elastic. Shape the dough into a ball and place on a tray with a light sprinkling of flour and cover with a damp cloth. Leave to rise somewhere warm for 30 minutes.

3. Preheat the oven to 475 degrees.

4. Place the onion, garlic, tomatoes, olive oil, and oregano in a food blender until smooth and add salt and pepper.

5. Sprinkle a surface with flour; roll the dough ball into a circle until ¼ inch thick.

6. Spread the tomato sauce thinly and evenly across the base.

7. Sprinkle a layer of cheese and arrange your toppings. Bake for 8-10 minutes until golden brown.

FOR A REALLY **FIERY** TASTE, SIMPLY ADD MORE PEPPERONI, CAJUN SPICE, AND PEPPERS. ENJOY!

ACKNOWLEDGMENTS

Killer Pizza is my first book, and I'm happy to be able to acknowledge some special people.

Beth Polson heard this story first and helped bring it alive. Dan Vining was a constantly inspiring guide as I worked on draft after draft of the book.

I'm fortunate that Scott Miller, my agent, not only decided to take on a new writer, but also, in Feiwel & Friends, found the perfect home for the KP manuscript. *Killer Pizza* is a better book because of Jean Feiwel's instincts and input, and the very helpful and specific notes of my editor, Kathryn McKeon.

Ben Pert provided the recipe that is included in the book. I tried out Ben's recipe before submitting it to F&F and can attest to how tasty Fiery Dragon-Breath Pizza is. Bon appétit, Ben!

A heartfelt thanks to my mom and dad. Among

other things too long to list, my parents allowed me to become the person I needed to be, and for that, I'll always be grateful.

Finally, I'd like to thank my family. I doubt that I would have started writing stories for younger readers had it not been for my son and daughter. Jessica and Ian, you continue to be the bright lights in my life. As does my wife, Joanne, whose rock-solid support through our many years together has meant the world to me.